ACCLAIM FOR
M. G. VASSANJI

"Vassanji probes beneath the surface to create a compelling and poignant portrait of human displacement." – *Ottawa Citizen*

"One of the country's finest storytellers." – *Quill & Quire*

"Vassanji's prose is simple and evocative, with a light touch he recreates places and times, deploying flashes of colour with a careful attention to detail." – *Financial Times* (U.K.)

"One of the most impressive voices in postcolonial literature." – *Canadian Literature*

"[Vassanji] writes in an inviting, straightforward style laced with humour. . . ." – *Vancouver Sun*

BOOKS BY M. G. VASSANJI

The Gunny Sack (1989)
No New Land (1991)
Uhuru Street (short stories, 1992)
The Book of Secrets (1994)
Amriika (1999)
The In-Between World of Vikram Lall (2003)

M. G. VASSANJI

UHURU

STREET

EMBLEM EDITIONS
Published by McClelland & Stewart Ltd.

First published in the U.K. by
Heinemann International Literature and Textbooks
Trade paperback with flaps published 1992
First Emblem Editions publication 2004

National Library of Canada Cataloguing in Publication

Vassanji, M. G.
Uhuru Street : short stories / by M. G. Vassanji.

ISBN 0-7710-8726-8

I. Title.

PS8593.A87U5 2004   C813'.54   C2003-906714-9

We acknowledge the financial support of the Government of Canada
through the Book Publishing Industry Development Program and
that of the Government of Ontario through the Ontario Media
Development Corporation's Ontario Book Initiative. We further
acknowledge the support of the Canada Council for the Arts and the
Ontario Arts Council for our publishing program.

This is a work of fiction. The community described, and the characters
in it, are fictitious, as are the events of the story. Any resemblance to
persons living or dead is purely coincidental.

My thanks to Ellen Seligman and Natalie Warren-Green for their patience and
time; and to the Ontario Arts Council and the Canada Council for support.

SERIES EDITOR: ELLEN SELIGMAN

Cover design: Terri Nimmo
Cover image: © David Turnley / CORBIS / Magmaphoto.com
Series logo design: Brian Bean

Typeset by M&S, Toronto
Printed and bound in Canada

EMBLEM EDITIONS
McClelland & Stewart Ltd.
The Canadian Publishers
481 University Avenue
Toronto, Ontario
M5G 2E9
www.mcclelland.com/emblem

1 2 3 4 5   08 07 06 05 04

For My Mother

Contents

Foreword

Dar es Salaam is a city on the east coast of Africa, a coast that over the centuries was visited by Arab, Indian, and European: traveller and merchant, slave trader, missionary and coloniser. Some 50 miles away on the Indian Ocean lies the former metropolis and slave market of the area, the isle of cloves, Zanzibar, barely visible on a clear day by some accounts. In 1498 Vasco da Gama stopped for rest and provisions on the coast, and took two guides along. His object lay across the ocean, beyond the horizon to the north and east, India: several weeks' journey by dhow when the Trade Winds allowed, later two weeks by steamer, now a few hours by plane. Dhows from Cutch and Kathiawad brought Indian traders here. In 1885 when Karl Peters began signing up the land around Dar for the German emperor, there were already small Indian settlements dotted along the coast.

Once upon a time Uhuru Street was called Kichwele Street. The change marked a great event in the country. *Uhuru* means 'independence'. This street of independence ran through the city. It began in the hinterland of exclusively African settlements, came downtown lined by Indian shops, and ended at the ocean. Here, where ocean liners came from distant lands, where a German ship was sunk to prevent a British warship from coming up close, where dhows once brought traders from Cutch and Kathiawad and Oman when the Trade Winds allowed, where the new quays were named after Princess Margaret after the old ones were destroyed by fire, Uhuru Street met the world.

Over the years Uhuru Street changed its looks; so did Dar, so did the country. The stories in this volume are about the Indians of Uhuru Street during these years of change.

The Dar es Salaam of these stories is a place in the world of fiction. But it *is* the real Dar es Salaam, just as it is also the other towns there, on the coast and beyond, through which Uhuru Street runs and seeks access to the world.

UHURU

STREET

In the Quiet of a Sunday Afternoon

Sunday afternoon languor descends over the street as usual. The day is hot but clear and a soft breeze blows bits of paper about. The street gradually empties of people and business comes to a halt. The last strains of Akashwani on the airwaves from India mingle with the smell of hot ghee, fried onions, and saffron that wafts down from people's homes. Hussein, my father-in-law, sits on the bench and stares out through the doorway, as intently as though watching some action on the pavement. In his hands are the two halves of a ball, a soft bouncy red ball, the kind kids call flesh-ball, and he squeezes the two parts together.

A short while ago the ball fell from a roof three floors up, bounced a few times on the street and pavement and landed inside the store. Hussein was upon it even before I realised it was there. Minutes later some boys came in, with a side of wood, their bat.

'Uncle, did you see a ball fall here somewhere?' they asked.

'Pigs!' yelled Hussein, jumping up from his seat in rage. 'Do you want to hurt people? *How* many times do you have to be told . . . ?'

'We won't do it again, uncle,' pleaded a boy.

'Pigs from hell! I will show you . . . devils!' He brought out a large knife and sliced the ball in two. A bit of rubber fell to the ground. 'Here,' said the old man, 'take this –' They looked at what remained of their ball in his hands and ruefully left the shop.

The boys call him 'German,' because, he says, he can speak

1

German. I've heard him say two things, 'Mein Herr,' and 'Mein Gott,' which I presume are German. He was still a youth when the Germans were here, and when he's in the mood he can spin quite a yarn about those times. We all have a name here. They think I don't know they call me 'Black.' Because I'm dark, almost an African. They have to give me a name, and what better name than something so obvious. Black. My wife is 'Baby', the whole town calls her Baby, and you have to see the rolls of blubber hanging on her to see why. She was brought up on nothing but the purest butter, proclaims her mother proudly. 'Our Baby was most dear to us,' says Good Kulsum, whenever I need reminding of the good fortune that has come my way. How I landed in this situation is another story. I married to attain respectability, but right now I wonder if I've not had enough of it.

Now Baby and her mother sleep after the biriyani and I wait up, the shop half closed as usual. The quiet of the Sunday afternoon has always been mine – it is nice and pleasant in the shade and the town sleeps. I sit on the armchair and read the *Sunday Standard* column by column, and when I've finished and solved the puzzle set for children by Uncle Jim, and noted last week's winner, I have tea and wait for the woman to bring samosas. All this peace while they sleep and snore. But not today. Today German sits with me.

And the woman who brings samosas at four every Sunday will not come, today she catches the bus to go to her brother's town.

Her name is Zarina and she first came a few months ago and called out softly from outside, 'Brother, do you want samosas for tea?'

I looked up from the paper and gave a good look at her and said, 'Yes, I'll take a few.' She came in, a small dark woman, her shallow basket covered with a newspaper. I fetched a plate from inside and she squatted and counted out five samosas and spooned out the chutney. I looked at those firm and large hips, the tight bodice, and I felt my blood thicken, a tightening in my limbs. Oh, how

2

long since I had a good woman before my days of respectability began. What blubber I have to manipulate just to father a child. Her face was smooth and round, her hair long and wavy, tied at the back. What misfortune befell you, woman, that you are reduced to ferrying samosas, I thought. I looked into those dark shiny eyes and I touched her arm as I gave her the shilling.

She pulled it back and her eyes flared. 'Aren't you ashamed, brother? Just because I am a widow and I come unaccompanied doesn't mean that I am a loose woman! My boy is asleep and I didn't have the heart to wake him up.'

'Forgive me, sister,' I said. 'I was not myself.'

She prepared to go. 'Baby is asleep?'

'Yes. They're all resting.'

The following Sunday she brought her son, and every Sunday thereafter. He would sit on the doorstep, watching the empty street, and she would sit inside on the bench. Her husband had been a coal seller and had died suddenly of a fever. She had only recently rented a room in the old house across the street and lived with Roshan. This Roshan has a certain reputation for her free ways. In any case, Zarina made a living selling snacks which she prepared and her son Amin helped to bear from place to place. Amin was ten years old or so and a quiet sickly fellow, surprisingly fair, for the coal seller wasn't very fair either. I would look at him sitting on the step and wonder, How long before he takes to the streets, before he starts stealing and pimping . . .

◇

It turned out so that whenever we were out of bread in the morning, I crossed the street for fresh vitumbua. The door was always kept ajar there for customers, and I would walk inside into the dark and narrow corridor, at the end of which she sat beside the fire. There were three rooms on the left which I passed, closed with curtains. Zarina's face glowed like the coals and there would be a film of sweat on her face. The air was rich with a sweet smell

3

of frying and the ceiling was covered with soot. She sat on a low stool, her hair undone and wavy, the hem of her frock tucked in front of her. The dough would be ready by her side, yellow and yeasty, which she would pour with a ladle into the small woks in front of her. Then she would prod the contents and turn them with a long skewer until they were raised like little tummies, brown and crisp, sizzling in the oil, almost filling the woks.

Baby loves vitumbua and she could eat two at a time. I would watch as Zarina brought them out one by one, and Amin would get the first lot to take away and sell. When he was gone I would await my share. Roshan would bring tea, and the two women would start to kid me. 'You left Baby's side early today!' Once Roshan caught my eye at the door as I was leaving and said: 'You know, if you find it difficult at home, you can always come here!' There was suggestion in those eyes and a wickedness in that smile that could give your heart a flutter. At the far end of the corridor the flames glowed yellow and blue, the little tummies sizzled, and Zarina watched us, one hand on a skewer. Without a word I stepped outside into the brilliant morning sunshine.

◇

German's suspicions were aroused perhaps when he saw me give a shilling to the boy.

'Eh, Amin!' I called out one afternoon as he emerged with a few others from behind the store. He came in and stood in front of me, eyes shining and mouth open. 'What were you doing back there?'

'Why? Playing.'

'Don't take me for a fool! I too was your age once – shall I report to your mother?'

He knew I had him, but gave one more try. 'Tell me, then, what was I doing?'

'Smoking! And shall I also tell you what? Why, look at you – all bones you are and you want to burn your insides smoking cigarettes! Play cricket, play football –'

4

In the Quiet of a Sunday Afternoon

'We don't have a ball!'

I still don't know what exactly it was that made me do it. 'Here,' I said, 'take this – buy one and stay out of mischief.' I gave him a shilling.

It was at this point that German shuffled in.

'You know, bapa,' I told him, a little guiltily, 'it's a pity there is no playing ground around here. The school is too far and at the Khalsa ground the caretaker chases them away. Boys need room to play.'

'They are pigs, all of them.' He made for the bench and picked up the measuring rod.

I thought this was too much. 'Why, what have they done to you?' I asked, a little sharply.

But the man refused the challenge. 'I said they are all pigs,' he said simply, and with that we stared silently in front of us. Good Kulsum was out and at the back we could hear Baby commanding the servant in her thick husky voice. It was dull and hot outside, few customers came in, and you wondered how long the lull would last. A little later, towards evening, things picked up. Baby puffed in and Good Kulsum stepped in exhausted from her rounds. German stood up and went out for a stroll and I was glad to see the back of him. Customer traffic picked up. Kulsum sang hymns in her grating toneless voice, counting beads from the bench, Baby served the customers and I gave out change and helped with wrapping. Baby is good with customers. She walks them in from the door, chatting amiably with them, and sees that they walk out with at least a good feeling if not something more.

That night she was angry and hurt.

'One whole shilling to someone we hardly know!' She looked at me reproachfully as she applied a generous layer of butter on a thick slice of bread, spread jam over it and handed it to me. Good Kulsum looked mournfully at me as she poured me my tea, and

German smirked, slurping over his bread over which he had poured his tea.

'We should be charitable to our neighbours,' I said in defence. 'We should do things for each other.' At which Baby and Kulsum remained silent, and the old man let out a series of muffled grunts through his skull, until I was forced to murmur, 'Watch it, bapa, the bread does not get into your brain.' And Kulsum looked more mournful than ever.

One morning he shuffled in as I sat kidding with the two women, sipping tea and watching the vitumbua frying in their woks.

'Indeed,' he muttered, 'one also gets tea while one waits!'

'Oh yes, bapa,' I said, 'have a seat, have a seat. Roshan, bring my father-in-law a chair!' You would have thought I owned the place.

'I have no intention of sitting,' said the man testily. 'I have a home. If it takes this long to cook vitumbua here, we can go elsewhere.'

The two women eyed each other. 'Go,' Zarina then said. The old man stood watching the fire.

'You are the daughter of Jamal Meghji,' he said at length.

'Yes,' said Zarina.

German loudly cleared his throat as if he were about to spit on the floor, then shuffled off to the door, stuck his head out and spat.

'I knew your father,' he said when he returned. 'What town was he from?'

'Mbinga,' she answered.

'I know that! Where in India?'

'I don't know. In Cutch or Gujarat somewhere.'

'Mudra,' he said, nodding at me. 'I remember when he came to Africa.'

She said nothing.

6

'Third class family,' he told me, as we came out with our basket of vitumbua. 'You know how he made his money?'

'They were rich, then?'

'He bought stolen goods. Flour and sugar. Then he sold it back. To the Germans. In one year, when the Great War in Europe began, he made all his money. And at the end of the war he lost it.'

'How?'

'Ah!' His mood changed as we approached the shop, and he waved away my question. 'But remember,' he said, 'third class family.'

◇

That night after supper he told the story. The table lay uncleared and we all sat around, waiting for someone to start something. First he burped, and then he asked his question, which is his way of starting a story.

'How did Jamal Meghji lose his wealth, Kulsa?'

'I don't know, it was all so long ago,' Good Kulsum murmured.

'Listen, then.' He looked at me. 'In the year 1916 a rumour went around that the Germans were losing the Great War, in Europe and even here. And with that rumour went another little rumour that the German soldiers were going around looting the businesses. People started hiding their cash and their jewellery, burying it and stuffing mattresses. Some other time I'll tell you what I did. This is what Jamal Meghji did. He had a lot of cash, ten thousand rupees, it was said. Even for Europeans that was a lot of money.

'Outside his house was a large tree, from which hung six, seven beehives. In those days this was the custom among Africans. People kept beehives. And according to the custom, you did not go near other people's beehives. You could not touch them, no. So Jamal Meghji hid his money in beehives. And there it was as safe as it could be. He could go to sleep in peace.

'The Germans were losing the war. Some months later some

7

German troops camped about five, six miles from the village. One day early in the morning a few German soldiers set out in search of food. And when they saw the beehives hanging from the trees, they pointed their rifles at them and shot them down. Jamal Meghji's beehives came down with all his wealth in them. In this way the woman's father died a pauper.'

◇

On Sunday evenings we walk to the seashore. Always in the same order, Good Kulsum in the lead, then Baby talking loudly over her shoulder at me just behind her, and German bringing up the rear. And when the girls in pretty new dresses we pass on the road pull aside and giggle at our procession Baby gives them a good piece of her mind.

'What are you laughing at? – Khi-khi-khi . . . ! They think they are so beautiful. Look at the teeth of that one! She scares me, she does!'

At the seashore we drink coconut water, the old man buys peanuts, and we stroll for a while watching kids playing in the sand, boats bobbing up and down on the water, steamers coming into or leaving the harbour. We wave at the passengers when they wave at us and we wonder from what world beyond they could be coming, what country the ship's flag represents. The Goan church starts to fill up and we troop slowly home.

In that same order I was brought home after the wedding, a prize. The taxi we took from the railway station deposited us on the road outside the shop. Kulsum got out of the front seat, and Baby beside me on one side and German on the other opened their doors. Already a small group of bystanders had gathered and people came to stand at the doors of their shops pretending to be casual. The old man was haggling with the driver and Kulsum was at the door when Baby and I walked in. The servant brought the trunks behind us. Good Kulsum never misses such a chance. A shower of rice fell upon us at the doorstep as she greeted us in

8

the traditional way, cracked her knuckles against our heads for luck, and pushed sweets into our mouths. The African girls who had gathered to watch smiled with pleasure and shyness, saying 'Mr Bridegroom!' 'May this union be blessed with long life and many children,' Kulsum crooned with pleasure, as the bride and groom stepped on and cracked the clay saucers for more good luck. 'God give you a long and contented life together.' Then she sobbed. By this time German had arrived and angrily shooed the girls away.

I was an orphan half-caste when I married, mother black. I was brought up by an Indian family, half servant and half son, and the night following the arrival of Good Kulsum and German with their proposal, I was told to take it.

◇

The other day Amin walked into the store.

'Uncle, Roshan says she wants to talk to you.'

'What, now? What is it?' I asked a little anxiously. This Roshan is a little disconcerting.

'She says now, if possible.'

'Alright. Go. Tell her I'm coming.'

I told Baby to come and wait in the shop, and I crossed the road to find out what Roshan wanted. A most unusual request, this, but for her perhaps not so. I entered the dark corridor. The first room on my left was her sitting room and parlour. At the end of the corridor the fires were cold, but the broken-backed chair on which I sometimes sat was there. Inside the room, I sat on an old sofa with faded embroidered flower patterns, whose legs had been cut. A cup of tea duly came my way and Amin was dispatched to buy something. Roshan sat across from me at her dressing table and I realised that I was sitting there like one of her customers.

'You wanted to discuss something?' I began.

'Yes, I have something to tell you. You must have heard that Zarina is going to live with her brother in Mbinga.'

'No, I haven't heard. What happened? Can't she make it here?'
'No, it is difficult. And the boy is giving her a hard time. He
needs a father. A man he can fear and respect.'
'Yes, yes. His uncle will be good for him.' I felt a little
uncomfortable. Behind her a faint light poured in through a small
window almost blotted with dust. She was slurping tea. 'She is a
good and clever woman,' I ventured warily. But you, I said in my
mind, are the equal of ten ordinary men.

'If you were a bachelor, you would marry her, I know!' And she
laughed merrily, her cup tinkled against the saucer. 'Why don't
you take her for your second wife?'

'This is no time for joking, Roshan,' I answered severely. She
had me positively flustered.

'I am not joking, brother. You like her and the other day you
touched her in your shop. You should marry her! Go with her!'

I spoke gravely. 'I don't need a second wife, Roshan. I have
Baby, and I am satisfied.'

'Ho! Who says? Why don't you have children then, tell me! You
like this woman and you touched her. And she is good and fertile, I
tell you. Good and fertile! And she works hard, as hard as your
Baby. You know what they are saying about you? They say you
are henpecked. "Like her son," they say. "Follows her like a tail,
wherever she goes. No stuff! Hides in her armpits!"'

When I've had enough I've had enough. I got up. 'Who says
this?' I asked. 'Let them say it to my face. Let them dare to say it to
my face! Just once, I tell you! Do you hear me? Tell them to say it
to my face!' I told her what I thought of them, whoever they were,
and I left.

◇

Behind the rooms in the courtyard the servant irons the clothes
I've decided to take with me. They include the shirts and trousers
I brought with me and the wedding suit which was a gift from my
guardian, nothing that I received from here. Behind me stashed

10

away inside a shelf is a wad of money that I've surely contributed to earning and which they could easily earn at month's end. These two things, the clothes and the money, I would like to take with me in a small wooden trunk I bought for this purpose from a hawker. Soon Baby and Kulsum will get up and prepare for the Sunday walk to the seashore. It has to be soon. But German sits there like an old dog who's smelt something. He sits patiently on the bench, with the knife in one hand and one half of the sliced ball in the other. If I go, it will have to be with the clothes on my body and the few shillings jingling in my pocket.

Ali

When Ali came to work for us we were in the throes of domestic disruption. His predecessor had failed to show up after borrowing thirty shillings to add to what little remained of his salary at month's end, and for a few weeks we were at the mercy of a spate of temporaries who could not be relied on for their honesty or their work. My two sisters went to school like martyrs one day – box pleats ending ruinously half way down their pinafores – and suffered the expected barbs from their teachers. 'We were the town fools today!' raged Mehroon, as another temporary servant was paid his daily wage and told not to return. Another day my brother Firoz's shorts returned from the wash minus a shilling. Or so he claimed and was largely believed. Finally I, only in Standard I and therefore excused from the punctiliousness expected of the others, nevertheless came home one afternoon with a note complaining about my attire. It was obvious, we could no longer simply wait in the hope that a suitable and cheap houseboy would happen by and set us in order once more.

Mother summoned Omari, the tailor at Parmar's Tailoring Mart nearby, who moonlighted sometimes by sewing our school uniforms and other clothes. Yes, he said, his brother was in town and looking for work. The next morning he brought Ali with him; the Ali who stood somewhat diffidently before Mother's doubtful gaze from her position on the high stool behind the counter. 'Same mother, same father?' was her first question, it being the common

12

belief that among the Africans the definition of brother – or
mother, or father, for that matter – stretched somewhat to suit
occasions.

'Ah, Mama, you jest!' laughed Omari good naturedly. 'He is the
son of my younger mother – he's my brother, no doubt!'

This belied appearance. The two could not have looked more
different. Beside the tall and stately Omari, in his clean white
muslin kanzu over his black trousers and checked red shirt, his
hand-stitched cloth cap, and his sandals, stood a proper mshamba
– a man from the farms, from the interior. Short, though thin, with
ruffled, thick hair, and barefoot – toenails broken, soles fissured
where they turned up, like those of someone who has never worn
shoes even under the hottest sun. Ali was coal black, and beside
him Omari could even pass off as fair. His cutoffs were in tatters,
his shirt had no buttons and was tied in front in a knot. He looked
sullen and gave mumbling answers to Mother's pointed questions.
But he looked honest, if only for his oafishness. You could not
easily mistake him for one of those shifty characters who made a
living by unpegging some item hanging for sale in a crowded store
and making a dash for it. For this reason, on recommendation, and
with no other choice, Mother hired Ali.

One more village boy would have to be house-trained. And after
that, how long would he last? If he was smart enough, he would
pick up the requisite skills and sooner or later move on to
employment in a richer home, finally even with a European family
– who could tell? We all wished though that we could afford the
well-trained servants who could run a household as smoothly as a
well-oiled machine, without being visible. As Grandmother's
Chagan and Magan did. Her servants, she said, were gems.
Everyone agreed. You only had to go to her home to see what a
good servant could do. She got their nicknames from the old ditty
that runs, 'My Chagan and Magan are of gold . . .' Their cooking
was famed: on rare occasions she would loan them for a commun-

13

ity feast. Everyone knew then that the feast would be something special. Remtibai's Chagan and Magan were cooking it. Her grillings of prospective servants were also legendary. Can you sweep? she would ask a nervous applicant. Can you do beds? Can you cook biriyani? Come on, tell me how! My sons, when they return from work, require a clean house, like those of the Europeans. Do you clean latrines? Yes Mama, yes Mama, yes Mama, he would answer; and then, only if she liked him, she'd come out with: 'And can you steal?' catching his 'Yes Mama' with a mischievous glint in her eye before he could quite suppress it.

But our Ali caught on fast, barring the first few days of anxiety and amusement: as when, at Firoz's suggestion, he tried to sip hot tea from the spout of the teapot to taste it for sugar; or, again at a similar suggestion, when he stood expectantly holding up the plug of the electric iron in his outstretched hand, imagining the electricity to flow from his body to heat the iron. On this second occasion it was only when Mother asked him rather sharply, 'But what are you *doing*, standing there like that?' that he realised something was out of order. But such incidents became rare, and soon everybody depended on him. His appearance changed too, and for the better as it only could. Gone were his initial surliness and embarrassment. He turned out to be of a more cheerful and lively disposition than we could have guessed.

At six every morning we woke up to his fist banging on the door. He would make the tea and send us off to school. Then he would clean the dishes, sweep the floors, and do the beds, before going down to help Mother who was already in the store. He would run errands and was learning to cook. Every evening a pile of clothes would be ready, washed, dried, and ironed – pleats done just right, shorts turned up at the legs at just the right length, shirt collars turned up or down, fully or partly, according to the dictates of current fashion in school. The pile rose in a pyramid from a chair, starting with a base of shorts and dresses and ending at the peak

14

with hankies. Each evening Mother would call out to him as he left, 'Tomorrow don't sleep, you hear?' And he, already outside, would reply, 'No Mama, I won't,' knowing full well what she meant.

In short, Ali became indispensable. Yet he showed no signs of wanting to move on. No backtalk from him, no laxity in his work. And herein lay the wonder. What kept him with us? Not the pay, certainly; and not the working conditions, for ours was a modest household, with no benefits to speak of. He did not steal: nothing was unduly missing from the flat; our curries prepared by Mother in the morning survived the day with their modest meat portions intact; and he faithfully took our food offerings to the mosque without consuming anything on the way, so we were assured by the chits he brought back with him. He could easily have found a better paying job elsewhere, now that he had mastered the workings of an Indian household. Neighbours were already eyeing him approvingly. But he did not leave. Everyone in our home appreciated this, of course, but it made the situation a little uneasy. There was a feeling of uncertainty about. Mother gave him a raise without his asking for it.

I was Ali's special and added responsibility. Often he came to fetch me from school when for some reason my elders failed to accompany me. On our way back, in the hot afternoon when the dirt roads and the whitewashed mud houses reflected sharply the sun's glare, when he saw me finally stumbling along and lagging behind, he would pick me up and carry me on his shoulders the rest of the way. He came looking for me when I was missed. And I used to plague him for the stories he knew. On our way back from school, or later across the table where I watched him iron clothes, or downstairs in the store when there was nothing special for him to do, I would plead with him: 'Say a story, Ali!' If he was in the right mood, his eyes would pick up a gleam, his face a smile. He would begin. He spoke about the cunning rabbit who tricked the

15

hyena; how the zebra exchanged his muddy brown suit for the lion's striped black-and-white; of wily Abunawas, who outwitted everyone in sight. As he went on his voice gained expression, his eyes caught fire, and I listened spellbound. 'The rabbit ran, and he . ran, he ran and he ran, he raaaa . . . an, until he got tired. Then he spotted a big leafy tree.' And Ali, himself getting out of breath, would drop whatever was in his hands and show the full expanse of the tree, its girth and height, and point to its top where the rabbit climbed, while his witless pursuer waited at the foot.

His favourite stories undoubtedly were about Shane. He had a host of Shane stories, most of which he invented as I now realise. A game he loved to play was to move to one side after knocking on our door. Then, when the door opened, he would step out swiftly with the cry, 'Shane, look out!' pretending to draw a revolver and shoot down whoever it was who had answered. Once he did that to Mother – by mistake, I believe – much to his dismay.

I learnt about Roy Rogers from Ali. On a wall in our stairwell he had drawn with charcoal a full-length sketch of the cowboy in full regalia. It was so well done that no one thought to bring him to task for defacing the wall, and no one ever wrote or painted over it. It stayed intact for years, long after he had left.

Thanks to him I had my first glimpse of royalty. The arrival of Princess Margaret in our town was an occasion for a big and lively celebration. Preparations were in progress for months, and the last few weeks before she arrived were like the days of festive Ramadhan. Streets were crowded, especially in the evenings. Stores, decorated with light series and flags, stayed open late and busy. Groups from schools, churches, Red Cross, and RSPCA, individuals on stilts and in fancy dress banging drums and tambourines, went around for donations. School bands, the police band, and neighbourhood bands equipped with lead pipes and tin-can maracas practised in different parts of the town. All of a sudden Union Jacks became a common sight, fluttering in rows on storefronts and in the hands of schoolchildren. Vendors of sweets, coffee, and brightly coloured sherbets set up on street corners or went about from store to store calling out their wares, whistling. The sounds of children playing rang out in the streets late into the evening.

Schools went through special preparation and drill for the royal visit. But to my great disappointment only the higher forms were to be allowed to welcome the princess. I missed the excitement of the rehearsals, the free lunches and sodas. Developments in the rehearsals were announced daily at home by Mehroon. She was the eldest and not for nothing called 'Reporter' by us. So and so would participate in the gymnastics display, someone else had the chance to sing the anthem, a third one would present a gift. Curtsies were demonstrated in our sitting room with much discussion and debate. I watched all this from a distance, feeling left out and envious. All the excitement seemed to be passing me by. On the day of the visit, even the motorcade was rerouted to miss our street.

Then, on the afternoon of the fated day, while I sat in the store with Mother and Ali and my younger brother Aloo, waiting for Mehroon and the others to return, a sudden commotion rose up in the street outside. A thunder of bare feet thudded down the street, as almost everyone who could simply left what he was doing and started running with excitement like a being possessed. Ali walked out, squinting at the sunlight, made a quick enquiry and hurried back inside. On the store bench he left the shirt he was working on and was off.

'What's up, eh Ali?' I shouted after him, looking up from an assembly of cardboard box and wooden reels on the floor.

'The young queen,' he said, 'she's coming!'

He stopped, came back inside, pulled my hand and together we took off. But that was no way to beat the crowd running with us, and soon I was on his shoulders, bumping along and towering over the others. We ran on main roads and along side streets, all the while following the crowd ahead of us as they took first this turn and then the other. Men and women came out of houses and stores, shielding their eyes from the sun, gazing towards a mass of people now converging from many directions. Some looked up at the sky and pointed. Finally we stopped where a huge crowd had gathered around the war memorial, the elevated bronze statue thrusting a bayonet at some unseen enemy.

'There it is – the bird,' said Ali, pointing up. And there it was, like a locust buzzing in the air – the helicopter from which the princess had landed. For some, as for Ali, this was the only sight they had of the royal presence.

Sitting on Ali's shoulder and looking over the black, fuzzy heads of the mass of people, all straining their eyes and craning their necks, I saw the princess waving a white-gloved hand. Her dress was white and her wide-brimmed hat was also white. A figure of such grace and poise, as if an angel had descended from the sky. And beside her, in his tasselled black and gold ceremonials, the Governor, Sir Philip Morrisson – a name whose each syllable we had learnt to pronounce with mystical awe.

Much as I liked Ali, and despite our special relationship, it was I who proved my elders right and caused Ali to leave us. There *was* something else for him in our home.

Every afternoon, at about three o'clock, Ali would leave the store and go upstairs to the flat to make tea and bring it down in a thermos. Mother was practically addicted to tea, which she required in regular doses. Without it her headache would creep up on her, paralysing her and causing the rest of us much anxiety. But Ali never had to be told – the tea was there when she needed it. It was one more reason that made him so special.

One afternoon Mother ordered me to go up after Ali to remind him to make an extra cup for my aunt who would be visiting. Grumbling, I went upstairs as I'd been told. When I reached the

Ali

landing the door was open. This was normal, of course – Mehroon was inside, and a girl did not lock herself up with a man, let alone a servant. But as I walked in, a strange and at first comical sight met my eyes, the meaning of which took me a while to realise.

Ali stood perched somewhat precariously on the large wooden dining table which he had moved. He was leaning against the top of the bathroom door and, face pressed against the metal bars, was looking down through the ventilator window above it at my sister Mehroon taking her afternoon bath. Upon hearing me, he started, looked at me, and jumped lightly down on the floor.

'I shall marry her,' he said, as if confidingly, and moved the heavy table back.

Ali was dismissed immediately, and Mother went without her tea that day. I never saw him again. Perhaps he went back to his farm, but more likely he found better employment elsewhere, possibly even with a European family. He was followed by Elias, more sombre, solid, who was not as good, but who stayed longer.

Alzira

The Jiwanis moved away to better times and places, all ten of them, and the four Pereras moved into the flat across the street. They brought to the place an air of gloom and depression such as it had not seen before. Soon afterwards Mrs Daya their neighbour reported to Mother: 'They come with a secret to hide.'

Each morning Mrs Daya descended on the street from the second floor, and did her rounds of the stores, while waiting for the fruit and vegetable sellers to arrive. She brought the freshest news and gossip. But the Pereras were Goans and their affairs of little interest to the rest of us. They would have passed through the neighbourhood without much notice, but for Alzira.

She walked into the store late one afternoon – school over and the family noisily crowding the customer space – holding a piece of printed material with a gleaming, threaded needle sticking out from it. With the other hand she moved aside a clutch of belts hanging from the doorway. A tall ambling girl with a large mouth and short, straight hair, her long faded dress hanging loosely on her. She was grinning, a little shyly.

'How are you, Mama?' she said. 'I live across the street, over there, and I sew ladies' clothes. I charge ten shillings for a dress, but for the first one I will charge seven. When you have something, let me know.'

Mother looked at her from behind the counter and the rest of us continued to stare at her.

Alzira

'I do all the modern styles,' Alzira told her, with a glance at my sisters. 'Look . . .'

She had two pattern books under the material and Mother's interest was caught. She took the books and flipped a few pages expertly until her eyes fell on a design.

'Look,' she said to my sisters, 'the pina. Just like the one that European girl was wearing.' Any European woman who chanced by on our street was the subject of Mother's deepest scrutiny, as she watched out for new patterns.

Mehroon and Razia jumped up from their seats and went to look over Mother's shoulders, while Alzira looked around the store. She checked the babies' bonnets hanging in a bunch, made by my grandmother, then the knickers, and the dresses on the rack.

'How would it look,' Mother asked, her finger on the pattern, 'if this line of buttons was removed, and instead you put a bow here – a chocolate-coloured bow?'

'Not bad, Mama. I've used a lace before, but a bow would look as good. Yes!'

With this piece of tact she won a place to sit. Aloo and I were asked to disappear – to play outside or study upstairs – and Alzira sat down on the vacated bench, throwing a sly grin of sympathy at us as we went out.

It became her regular place, this bench, in the late afternoons. Sitting, legs crossed and hunched over some material, needling away, chatting with Mother, or gossiping with Mehroon and Razia when they were back from school. Alzira's afternoon news – unlike Mrs Daya's morning bulletin – merely supplied merriment.

We learnt that Baby, who lived in the low tin-roofed house across the street, had been ordered by her husband to touch her toes one hundred times before dinner. Poor Baby couldn't even see her toes standing up. Alzira had simply listened in to the passionate quarrel taking place downstairs from her window. Next

21

we received confirmation of what had long been suspected. That Roshan Mattress, who owned the third store from ours, entertained a Punjabi police inspector as lover. He came around ten o'clock in the morning pretending to look for stolen goods. The two would disappear into the shadowy interior of the store, ostensibly searching piles of mattresses and diligently prodding stacks of stuffing as they inched their way behind them. They emerged noticeably chipper, ordering tea and snacks. The inspector would leave brushing lint from his uniform and swinging his baton.

Alzira cheered us up. Her company was a boon to Mother, and she made the girls blush and giggle. Only as the afternoon drew to a close, after a cup of tea from the thermos that stood by Mother's feet, or having been treated to bhajias from Khatibai's Saidi who came around on a bicycle, would she gather up her things and take her leave.

What we learnt of her own family we also found out through gossip and observation. Her father was a retired civil servant, a big morose man, flushed and balding, whom we usually saw in khaki shorts and hanging shirt tails. Except on Sundays he rarely ventured out for long, going only for a paper or, it was rumoured, a bottle. The mother was a thin sickly creature, prematurely old and with dark uneven teeth, who came out on even rarer occasions. Alzira had a brother and sister, both younger and educated. Pius worked in customs at the harbour, and Maria – small, dark, vivacious – was a secretary with a law firm. They were regulars at the Goan Institute, these two, where jazz trumpets blared on Saturday nights and boys with Elvis hairstyles and girls in cancans did the rock 'n' roll. On Sundays Alzira walked to church with her mother and father, curbing her naturally long strides to allow them to keep pace. Maria usually got a ride, and Pius went off with some friend on his scooter.

I dreaded being sent to Alzira on errands. Her mother invariably answered the door, her black teeth and bad mood giving her the look of a snarling witch. Motioning me to wait she would go back in, while I stood outside in the littered landing for her daughter to come and see to me.

A long and dark passageway led inside, into whose mysteries I could not see and was not let in to see. But I discovered my own access: our second-storey window looked down into their three rooms facing the street. And sometimes, with nothing else to occupy me I would be drawn to that window. I looked on, unashamedly, observing the uneventful workings of that other home; long minutes of staring deep into that gloom, temple pressed against the cool metal bars. Scene after scene of silent, meaningless activity, as if carried out by phantoms. Lights on in one room; a newspaper fetched, a dress material picked up from a chair; lights off, then on in the next room; someone reading, someone sewing, someone drinking long from a glass. Rarely more than a person in a room, rarely a scene of hilarity or mirth. Sometimes the lights never turned on, and the grey evening shadows were engulfed by the black night without a protest.

◇

The news of Maria's engagement passed like a ripple through the neighbourhood. For the brief period of a few days it went around, was marvelled at and commented upon and then allowed to pass, pending developments. Maria was not liked very much for her high and mighty (it was thought) ways and the news while it lasted was a cause for envious backbiting.

We learnt from Alzira that Maria had gone to visit an aunt in Kericho in Kenya, where she met the man she got engaged to; and (from Mrs Daya) that the aunt had made several prior phone calls and the engagement had all the appearance of being 'arranged.' Mrs Daya had the only telephone in their building. Maria's fiancé (or 'lover' as he came to be called) was the only son of a rich family, and it was this that was the cause of all the excitement and envy. He lived with his mother and sister on a European tea estate that he managed. What he offered was nothing less than a release for Maria – a release from drab surroundings into the high and good life of garden parties, travels abroad and chauffeur-driven trips to Nairobi.

While the news was still fresh Maria herself arrived – the triumphant queen returned – not too unwilling to show herself more now while she waited and shopped for the big day. An announcement duly appeared in the *Sunday Standard*, accompanied by a picture of the couple. Maria had all the luck it seemed.

It was then that Mother came out with her advice to Alzira and told her not to take things too lightly.

'You should also get married,' she pronounced one afternoon.

Alzira deftly snapped the sewing thread from the material on her lap and smiled, retying the loose end.

'I'm in no hurry Mama . . .' she said, 'I will bide my time. I don't want to marry any old person and regret it for the rest of my days!'

'Don't be too choosy. It will be too late then. There is nothing like having a man of your own, I tell you. Even if he be one-eyed or lame – a man is a man.' She nodded knowingly. 'Without a man you'll be nothing. Haven't you had any good offers?'

Alzira grinned in embarrassment, finally looking up from her sewing. All eyes were on her.

'There must have been *some*,' said Razia. 'Tell us about them . . . Come on, tell us! Please!'

Razia and Mehroon had reached fifteen and sixteen, and marriage and boyfriends had become subjects of keen interest. Only recently a young man had started spending time at our store, treating everyone to Coke and roasted mhogo and being a lot of fun – until Mother found out that he'd been boasting about his exploits with Mehroon that he had obviously made up. He was told, with much loss of face on his part, that her daughters were not ready for marriage yet and he never showed up again.

24

'Well, there was this teacher . . .' Alzira began.

'Who?' said several voices at once. All the teachers in town were known.

'John Fernandes . . .'

'Fahndo? What are you saying! Really? *Mr* Fernandes?'

Mr Fernandes, or 'Fahndo', taught history at the boys' school and had a reputation for his arrogance. He rode a scooter, spoke good English, and was turned out rather smartly. He also knew his subject which was not always true of our teachers, especially those who came from India and Pakistan. The thought of Alzira saddled behind Fahndo, holding him by the waist, was on several minds at once. She was a head taller than he.

'Did he give you rides?' asked Razia.

'Yes, several times!'

'Then what happened?'

'His family thought I was too tall – and not educated enough.'

'How stupid!' said Mehroon. 'If he thinks himself so educated and modern, why does he stop to listen to them?'

'In these matters all men are old fashioned,' said Mother.

'What about the others?' asked Razia.

'Oh!' Alzira got up. 'Next time – I'll tell you about them next time!'

'There were many then?'

'Yes, lots!'

'How old do you think she is?' Razia said to no one in particular when Alzira had left.

'Twenty-five,' Mehroon said knowingly.

'Mummy, do you think it's too late for her?'

'It all depends on her kismet,' Mother answered broodingly, picking her chin. 'She will get whatever's written for her, good or bad.'

We knew what she meant – birth, marriage, and death were

preordained, as she often said. You had many choices in life: but not with these three.

When next time Alzira came down and was cornered we found out that there had been only one other suitor. A dealer in tusks and hides, she said, who operated from Goa. He wrote to her in a long sloping hand, as she showed us. But she didn't believe he would come for her. 'He can't leave his old mother, you see,' she said. My sisters tried to convince her that she should go and fetch him herself.

'No, no,' she said, 'I've given him up.' She looked at me with a smile and announced: 'I'll wait for *him* to grow up!'

'Take him now,' Mother said, 'I've had enough of him!'

I liked Alzira and was flattered by her remark. There was something in her that deeply touched me and warmed me to her. She was plain but jolly, and deep, kind, not frivolous.

◇

All of the two months allowed for Maria's engagement passed without the wedding date being set. The flurry of activity which had begun to enliven their home subsided, and then the preparations ceased altogether. People stopped asking questions. Roshan Mattress humphed when she passed Alzira, and Maria was not to be seen. 'Gone to become a nun,' Mrs Daya reported. 'Gone to visit our aunt,' said Alzira. She admitted that the wedding had been called off. The man's mother had been against it all the time. 'It's all for the better, he was too much under her influence,' she said.

It was Sunday afternoon and Mother was waiting for Alzira to leave before giving the servant the signal to begin the elaborate preparations for closing. Sunday was half day and it was past the time. Mehroon and Razia were upstairs, cooking and cleaning, and only I was with Mother. There was a silence inside the shop, and Mother was staring out, deep in thought. Alzira was busy darning. At this point a sudden commotion arose outside on the pavement, with much shouting and laughing. 'Tembo-mbili-potea!' one voice called out, and then another.

Apparently Tembo-mbili was passing. He was one of Dar's several crazies, a small, thin Goan man. He had recently taken to passing our street on Sunday afternoons, dragging a foot and being jeered all the way by the Africans in the street. It was said that he had landed from a steamer in delirium one day, muttering 'Tembo-mbili-potea' – 'Two elephants lost.' The elephants, they said, only referred to the brand of beer that came with the picture of an elephant and the man was drunk, but the name stuck. He had close-cropped hair and always wore a crumpled and dirty 'khaki and white'. With downcast eyes he shuffled along, looking tired and docile. 'Tembo-mbili-potea!' men would jeer when he'd passed them, 'Tembo . . . mbili . . . poteaaa!' He would ignore them. After some time, his patience worn out, wearily and without a word he would pick up the closest large stone he could find and hurl it at some offender. He would have made a mean fielder. He could throw cleanly across a block, from one end to the other, and the stone would land with a crash on the pavement, sometimes bouncing off walls and doors. No one dared to tease him from up close.

But this time some bold rascal had stolen up behind him and hitting his arm had dislodged the stone from his hand. Tembo-mbili stood weaponless and flustered in the middle of a loud and jeering crowd outside our store.

'They'll beat him up!' I said frantically from the doorway and turned to look out again. As I did so I noticed Alzira's anxious face. She was straining to look outside from where she sat, unaware in her agitation that her needle was pressing her thumb. I continued to look out, uneasy and dejected.

A constable walked up and started dispersing the crowd. Then Alzira's brother Pius arrived stiffly on his scooter, drove it on the pavement and picked the unharmed man up, and without a word they rode off.

Alzira stood up and left, shaken, almost in tears; Mother and I stared after her and then looked at each other without a word.

The Beggar

He comes out from the shadows and stands beside the solitary
service pole at the corner and watches the boy intently. A stocky
old man in a checked loincloth and a tattered white T-shirt. His
face has a tough leathery texture and is wrinkled at the eyes. He is
black. Across the street the boy gets his change from the Arab
shopkeeper and walks away with a can of milk in one hand and a
Coke bottle in the other. The street is dark, except for the light that
falls from the shop; a few pedestrians are about. The man watches
the boy's shape blur and enter the darkness which arrives before
the paved and lighted Kichwele Street further ahead. He takes a
few steps to follow and halts when the boy, as though afraid of the
dark, breaks into a run. Soon the patter of footfalls subsides and
the man walks back into the shadows.

A while later he emerges again and crosses the street to the
Arab's store. It has a wide serving window open to the street,
behind which its owner sits. 'Give me some water,' the man says
gruffly, standing outside. The owner looks up from behind a
kerosene lamp at the one-armed man and points to the red clay pot
at the doorway. The man shuffles to it. The Arab turns his gaze
outside once more. The radio, turned very low, gives the news
from behind him.

Having had his drink the man wipes his mouth with the back of
his hand and starts walking towards the main street, whose
pavements will be kinder to his feet. The night is warm and the air

29

is still. The shopkeeper watches the stocky figure disappear in the dark, holding a cane in the one hand.

Last night the one-armed man saw the boy escorting his older sister on Kichwele Street. He followed, keeping his distance. The girl walked fast and the boy had trouble keeping up. He tried talking, to slow her down, but she kept her pace and the boy had to trot along beside her. Finally they reached an open store, where he left her and then retraced his way back. Hands in his pockets, face turned downward, kicking stones on the pavement. For a moment the man thought their paths would finally cross, he would get his prey. His face tensed up and set into a wry bitter smile, his eyes gleamed. But then the boy started walking along the road behind parked cars and in a quick motion crossed to the other side. A bus hurtling along and two cars later the man had lost his quarry, who disappeared in the shadows of the buildings across. He turned back.

I will get him. I will get this chubby Indian boy even if I have to walk this street up and down every day . . .

At regular intervals green government trucks suddenly appeared in the main streets at night and a general chase ensued, policemen jumping out and checking African pedestrians for their cards. Those who couldn't produce them were carted off to the police station, and if not claimed by employers the following day were sent off to their villages.

A month ago he had found his way back to the city after six months upcountry. And a few days later on the morning of Eid, he had come across the three boys, returning home from prayers, all in crisp, new clothes, polished shoes and slick hair. They were in a jolly mood. He stood aside to let them pass and stretched out his hand, respectfully, with a friendly grin. They took no notice, continued to play. One of them tickled the other, the thin, bony one, at the sides, who turned around with a shout and gave chase. The two boys ran around a parked car several times, chasing and provoking each other in turns. The chubby one stood back, calling after them and laughing.

The man stood watching, ignored and hurt. Then in a final effort, he turned on the grin and started walking towards the chubby one, his only hand held out once more to beg. The cane protruded upwards and sideways from the hand. The boy, doubled up in excitement and pleasure, saw the raised cane and the man's grinning face and straightened up. With a look of terror he let out a cry and started to run. The other two gave up pursuit of each other and with a look at the man, followed. The man stopped in his tracks and watched them. Then, in a fit of anger he ran after them, giving them a good chase for a few hundred yards. They jumped over gutters, pushed aside people and ran into each other in their fright. They kept running even after he had stopped and turned back exhausted.

What cowards they are, these Banyanis. Three boys like that . . . and an old man like me. Even their fathers – all faggots. Hanisi! When I was young I stopped them, walking home nervously across Mnazi Moja Grounds. A gruff 'Give me money' and a shove in the chest was enough to produce a coin . . .

Two weeks after he first chased the three boys, he came across one of them again. Not the chubby one, or the bony one who got tickled at the sides, but the other, the sly one. This time he was walking along Selous Street which goes straight up to the school. It was late afternoon, school was over and the boy was walking home alone in the opposite direction, swinging his satchel. The man did not recognise him at first. But a few yards ahead of him the boy stopped and giving him a fearful look crossed the road and started running. The man turned and gave chase. This time he ran farther, for a full mile or so, and he ran with all the strength he had. The boy took several corners but he followed. People sitting outside their houses, old men playing bao, looked up unperturbed. Several times the boy looked behind and tried to gather more speed to lose his pursuer. He was getting tired. Then he reached the potters' village and ran in through the gates. The man went and stood behind a small baobab tree, exhausted. His sides ached and his head pounded. The soles of his bare feet hurt and the stump which was his left arm throbbed with pain. A few minutes later an Indian woman came out through the gate, wiping her hot face with the end of her veil. She checked both ends of the road and then motioned the boy to come. The boy returned the glass of water and started walking home. The woman stood watching after him, glass in hand. The man did not follow.

Why do I scare them so? Am I the devil, now? Or a djinn?

A week later he saw all three of them again. Early in the morning at sunrise out for a stroll. They stayed in the middle of the street and moved away only when a car or a bus appeared. Chattering in low tones they first walked up the long Kichwele Street all the way to the seashore. They walked along the shore for some time, their voices louder, there being no residences there. Then they started walking back. By this time the sun was higher and there were people and cars on the road. On the way two of them started a fight. The chubby one and the sly one. They exchanged a few shoves and got ready with their fists. The bony one intervened. He pulled the chubby one aside and talked with him while the other looked away and sulked. Then the bony one and the sly one talked, and peace was made. They walked home in silence, the peacemaker in between. It was while following them back that morning that he found out where one of them, the chubby one, lived. At the corner of Kichwele and Livingstone Streets.

◇

It is evening. There are people on the pavements. The man is walking up Kichwele Street and the boys are returning home on the same side. They are talking excitedly in loud voices. When they reach the shoemaker's store they stop and chant something in unison and laugh. The shoemaker, sitting on the floor, his feet pressed to a shoe, waves a hammer and swears; the boys go on. Now their paths will cross, the man is sure. They are too much involved in themselves to decide suddenly to cross the street, or to see him walking in their direction. He keeps as much as possible in the shadow of the parked cars. The chubby one is to the outside. He sees the man at the same time as the others, only a few feet away. They start to run. The chubby one catches his foot in the broken pavement and lurches forward. The man, arm raised, brings down the cane heavily on the boy's left shoulder. The boy gives a loud howl and lands flat on his stomach. The man, whom they had made into a devil, walks on.

For a Shilling

She gives a loud masculine howl as the smouldering matchstick head disappears into the shadow and makes its shaky contact there.

'For one shilling you can give her the burn,' he had said. The burn. That mysterious infliction referred to by adults in brief parenthetical statements that ended with dark suggestive silences, leaving the mind to grope at its further reaches. I had not yet reached the refinement my friend Ahmed knew about. What kind of burn? I had often wondered, never having seen one given. A match? A nice brass spatula fresh from flipping a hot chappati? On the shins? The thighs? I was getting closer.

'Do you know what happens to girls who pee in bed?' he asked me one day.

I looked back squarely at him, without a word. Perhaps even with a challenge in my eyes. The trick in these instances is to appear knowledgeable. But inside I felt a tingle, a luxurious thrill run down me. Here was another of those deliciously dirty secrets he hoarded, which he shared with the adult world and let drop one after another in our outings.

'They get the burn,' he said. I maintained my calm. 'You know where?' Now his smug, derisive look told me something had been let out for me to catch.

'Don't tell me,' I said, unable to contain myself any longer, 'you mean there, in the – ' Then he made the proposition.

34

For a Shilling

From a bully who had laid ambushes for me at the bottom of the dark staircase of our building he became a friend and a mentor. And he laid down his guns and converted for that simplest of reasons: money. He taught me expensive tricks, at a shilling each, and I paid up. My price into the fantastic – and all too real – world he conjured up for me. A price for knowledge not easy to come by. Starting with simple revelations, and explications of what I knew only by hearsay and mouthed without understanding about our boys' world. The crazy world of our daily associations – of Arabs, Africans, Asians and assorted half-castes – in which the arse was king.

In our moments of rage, it was your arse this or your arse that. It was on the arse that the big boys patted you if you let them get too friendly, and Lord forbid you sit on a willing lap in a crowded car returning from school. Starting with the arse then and culminating in the burn, a weird introduction to that other, that hidden world. Of girls.

One day when our relationship was new and still uncertain, he said to me, 'You know, Amin sells.'

Amin was a cheeky, spoilt, rich kid, whose father Mzee Pipa owned the only motor car for a block. I looked silly.

'Heh? What does he sell?'

'His arse, stupid!'

I confess I still looked dumb. He was so much beyond me in such matters, and what he said so teased the imagination, that I was often, as they say, a 'tube light': blinking uncertainly.

'You don't believe me?' he said, excited and intimidating, as if ready to fight. 'Nizar and Ramesh – them. They have a hideout . . . and – I swear it, upon my mother!'

The recollection was too much for him and he doubled up in a fit of such loud laughter, snortles and backslapping that it brought tears to his eyes.

'They've got big fat ones you know,' he added, making a fat circle with thumb and forefinger.

I was aghast. He had bowled me over by the very concreteness of his disclosure, its closeness to our lives. Could *that* actually happen among people we knew? But that was Ahmed. With him things happened. He gave life to words. There was now a drumming in my ears and I would have given anything to find out more.

'You will see,' he said. 'Pipa's driver caught them at it yesterday – but they might also be there today. One shilling,' he added.

We got up from our hideout under the staircase, dusted our backsides and walked up to Pipa's courtyard across the street. There we sat behind an old rotting cupboard and waited, well concealed from the traffic of people that went up and down the stairs to the flats above. We would wait, he said, until we heard sounds from behind the wall. Then we would place the bricks and boxes against it, stand on top of them and look down on the action. We waited one hour and nothing happened. I thought I'd been had. With a story like that and no proof – well . . . I stood up and started walking.

'Give me my shilling,' he said. I refused.

'I told you about it, didn't I? I've shown you the hideout, haven't I?'

Still I refused. Whereupon he threw me to the ground and prised away the shilling from my now yielding fingers.

It was a rough world. There were only a few tough boys on the block, but you had to tame them or be terrorised. They could get you on the dark staircases or in the streets at night, or they could wait for you after school and harrass you on the long way back home. He was not any bigger than I: but there are some who are born fighters and others who just aren't. A big brother could help but I was the eldest boy in my family. I chose the old and time-

tested method of paying off. As the proverb goes, when trouble arrives, send it home with a penny.

My family had moved into the second floor of the most recent of the two-storey buildings that were giving a new, modern look to our side of Kichwele Street. Ahmed and his brother and sisters were on the first floor. Their grandfather was the landlord.

They were a brood of five orphans, three of whom could not speak but could let out loud horrifying yowls during quarrels. But in their saner moments they used gestures and made soft sounds that were almost a pleasure to hear. Then you could almost make out the words they struggled to dislodge so painfully from their mouths. To call them you hooted: 'Hoo!' as everyone did, and they responded. Their disability gave them ugly faces. The youngest was a boy of about seven, with a long face and a mouth he moved into a sort of twist when he tried to talk. Then came a sister, of about the same age, also dumb. Followed by Ahmed, and then the terror: Varaa. She was heavy and strong, with a large mouth and a wild look, frequently barefoot, and in a loose frock that was always too short. She was a terror for what she could do with that mouth: let out howls of anger – or sorrow, for she also cried – that sounded varaa, varaa, varaa! Hence her name. Just to avoid hearing this babel you would keep your distance.

The eldest was also a girl, of about sixteen, the most normal. She dressed neatly, went to school regularly and talked to neighbours – mainly to hear complaints about her brothers and sisters or to defend them. She defended them vigorously but could not manage them herself, and was often very much a part of the screaming and yelling that went on inside that flat. Sometimes she simply left them and went to live with relatives.

This was a family of howlers that periodically went berserk. They lived on the floor below us and we trod it with special care, gingerly, when a fight was in progress. It would not have taken

much provocation, so it seemed then, for the whole lot of them to stop fighting among themselves and to fall on you like a pack of hyenas. Accompanying the howls would be the sounds of objects getting thrown: chairs, spoons, pots and pans.

Periodically too – for better or worse it was always hard to say – the grandfather came to mete out punishment. He was a small thin man in a crumpled white drill suit and a black fez. He brought with him a cricket stump, held firmly at the spike with what seemed a certain urgency. When the door closed behind him the howls became ferocious, interspersed with the sounds of the old man's oaths. Downstairs in the street people would look up and pause, some knowingly, others in alarm.

I remember the first day we moved into that building. I had taken my two younger brothers up to the roof terrace to keep them from getting under people's feet. There we were, myself looking down on the traffic below, and these two youngsters making hopscotch markings with charcoal, and what happens but we get our first treat to the howling chorus: varaa, varaa, varaa.

She swept in through the doorway, trailed by her two youngest siblings, making emphatic gestures with her fat arms, thumping along from wall to wall, glaring at us. Then she came and stood in front of me, arms akimbo, eyes fiery. The message was clear: this was her territory. My youngest brother had started to cry, and my own hair stood on end. It was my first sight of her – let alone of a dumb threesome – and she looked wild. Slowly I walked past her and down the stairs with my two charges and this foretaste of things to come. What a way to move into a new home.

It was us and them. There were no other kids in the building, and they had Ahmed. Vocal, strong, a bully, a fighter; a loafer. The staircase was his domain. He would sit sideways on a step near the bottom, his feet stretched across it, daring you to jump over. Sliding down a balustrade he would call out names. At night the staircase was dark and menacing. When threatening sounds –

38

hoots and chortles and moans – issued forth from its shadows there was no doubt who lurked behind them.

He roamed the streets with a gang of boys, and he made threats about what they could do. He loved a fight. It would be nothing for him to take you into a hold from behind and make you fight or trip you. The school had given up on him, he came and went as he pleased. And like many bullies, he was an expert at marbles. It was sheer folly to play with him, however much he persuaded you, for he could make you 'serve plays' for a lifetime if he wanted.

We might have moved from that unholy place if some sort of unstable truce had not been declared between our families. And I take no small credit for that.

It started the following way. I had finished buying a cut-up chutneyed mango from the roadside on my way home from school and was putting back my five-cent change when he walked up to me. After school a row of hawkers squatted behind a display of wild or unripe fruit normally forbidden at home. Those who had the money bought, others borrowed, begged slices or bites, or hung around unfulfilled and drooling.

'Can I borrow five cents,' he said. 'I'll return it tomorrow.'

I then did one of the wisest things I've ever done; I said 'Goodbye, copper.'

He bought a mango with it and we walked back together. Thus began our dubious friendship, held together delicately with a reasonable supply of cash. For me began a period of revelations – of grisly little bits of information that shocked yet sent tingling sensations down my spine and left me yearning for more; of guilty knowledge: forbidden fruit. My bought prestige was duly recognised on the block – and became a cause for concern at home. I must confess that my life at home was one tedious drone. I was ruled by a triad of females – my mother and two older sisters – and I had, besides, one drip-nosed and another smart-arsed brother, both younger than I. My lot there was a series of long,

39

drawn-out sermons and sob stories of family misfortune handed
down in the evenings after dinner. And a call for more work and
help. Nothing exciting happened, life was a small cooperative.

That day, our first day of association, Ahmed invited me to join
him and other boys in their nocturnal revelry. So in the evening on
the way home from mosque, somewhat warily I passed by the
street corner he had indicated and watched them from a distance.
That gang of boys, I decided, I was not ready to join as yet. They
were a desperate lot, whose families – if they had any – had even
given up on them. I am cautious by nature. I decided I would have
my excitement in small, controlled doses. After all, I was going to
pay for it.

They sat on the steps of a store in darkness, visible collectively
as a dense shadow occasionally changing shape, emitting a
murmur or two, a cracking of fingers, a chuckle, and so on.
Occasionally too a match would strike then go off and a cigarette
glow travel from end to end. Then, when a pretty young thing
passed by, clop-clopping on the pavement and framed splendidly
by the light from the corner lamp post, they would begin with calls
and whistles. 'Sweet arse!' would go the cry, 'Oh my! Milky-milk-
white!' It took some nerve.

I related this one evening to my sisters, the two tyrants at home,
Mother's viziers. There was no end to surprises. I thought I was
saying something offensive, which would put Ahmed in a horrible
light (we'd had a fight), making him appear as the very devil
incarnate. Perhaps I hoped the old grandfather would hear about
this and bring his cricket stump to bear on that fat rump. But no.
They loved it! They made me repeat that incantation syllable by
syllable, to the very tones in which it had been chanted. 'Oh my!
Sweet arse! Milky-milk-white!' Talk about lack of excitement at
home.

To come back to the proposition. For a shilling I could give her
the burn, he said. I paid up. I obtained the shilling as I'd always

done; in the thick of end-of-month rush in the store, pretending to help and looking as busy as a bee, stationed behind the cashbox, I slipped the coin quietly into a pocket. I'd never been caught before, but this time brother Smartarse saw me and when I was outside the store, threatened to report.

There is one way to teach such kids a lesson. They trail behind you in school and all over town, expect you to protect them from other kids, and then play you off against your elders. I landed one resounding smacker across his cheek and off he went howling to report: but only the lesser crime. This obstacle overcome, I went off to where Ahmed awaited me at the staircase and placed the shilling in his sticky palm.

We went up and I followed him into the cave that was their flat. I had never been behind those doors before and I did so then with some trepidation. I looked behind me nervously as I entered. Inside, it was strangely quiet, and dark. The windows there, except for one or two of them, were always kept closed. Some of them were boarded up with boxtops and plywood. The curtains were drawn that afternoon and light was barely visible through them. I walked behind him without looking right or left in what I knew, from the plan of our own home above, to be the dining room. We turned right into a bedroom. There were three beds in it each alongside a wall. He made for the one to our right. I followed. In it was Varaa.

He started making signs with his hands, and the soft clucking half-words that only they understood. It seemed that she was in on the deal. She gave a grunt of annoyance and drew back her legs, bending them at the knees. He let her dress slip back and parted her legs further. Then he lighted a match and handed it to me. Shadows moved on the walls as he did so and our three silent figures emerged sharply in the dim orange glow of the fluttering light. I moved in with the flame. The darkness between her legs had disappeared to reveal fleshy brown thighs and a panty-less crotch covered lightly with a black fuzz. On her face was an anxious look – wild eyed, open-mouthed.

Suddenly he smacked the back of my hand and the match dropped to the floor; greyness returned.

'Put it out, stupid, and let it smoulder – or you'll burn her fuzz!' he yelled in irritation.

He lighted another match and handed it over. I waved it smartly in the air, once, and the flame died. Then sweating profusely in that dark and stuffy bedroom, with trembling hand and breath held back, as if trying to light a potentially explosive primus stove, I edged closer with the smouldering matchstick.

The Relief from Drill

For a few months Aloo brought a sense of plenitude to our lives. He made us taste from bounties which we had felt were beyond us. But at what a cost. A cost to himself in terms of the shame and humiliation, the fall from grace. And to myself, his elder by two years, dutybound to play the watchdog, the cold-blooded conscience that noted and faithfully reported.

The idea had perhaps entered his mind, that good things could be had cheaply and need not be bought in the expensive stores downtown, when my friend Azim brought home a gramophone from the mnada.

The mnada was an open-air market in the African section of town. It was a square bustling with activity, uproarious with catcalls and jeers and bargains being struck, festooned with brightly-coloured cloth and lit up in the night with the yellow light of kerosene lamps. It was packed in on three sides by rows of mud houses and accessible on the fourth by a short alley. As you came up this alley, missing potholes, avoiding banana and orange peels and other rubbish, giving right of way to carts of fruit and other wares pulled by men with impatient voices and straining backs, a brilliant and unsettling display of furniture suddenly came in sight. Folding chairs, sofas and tables, all functional – simple, roughly finished, varnished cheap red or gleaming yellow – lay exposed to the world and the weather. In front of this display, alongside the road and the open gutter ran a line of fruit and peanut sellers.

43

Behind the furniture in small make-shift stalls and spread out on racks, crates, and on the ground, were the other articles on sale: new and used clothes, shoes, glass beads, mirrors and plastic jewellery; Japanese perfumes with exotic-sounding Arabic names, in bottles that cracked if exposed to the sun; toys, and even used appliances. Many a common thief had been chased through these grounds. Music bands sometimes used the ready audience here to begin their rounds of the streets in the evenings.

It was while walking through this market, with no intention whatever of buying anything, that Azim and I were shown the gramophone, treated to a song, and then persuaded to buy it at a giveaway price. He was the more impressionable I believe. 'Wait here,' he commanded me in great excitement. 'I'm going home to get the money.' The loquacious vendor he silenced with 'Don't sell it, I'm coming right back!' Meanwhile I was given a stool to sit on and treated to the scratchy record one more time as we waited. It was called 'Ribbons and Things.' For the next few weeks we heard it over and over again, before Azim could induce his father to part with more money for a modern short-playing record.

The mnada was not a respectable place to shop in because of the type of people believed to hang around there – jobless Africans from the districts, and thieves. Boys sometimes went there in search of cheap things: footballs or cricket bats, in a last desperate bid to outfit a budding team. And then, popular belief had it, especially in the Indian shops, that the newer and more decent articles there were 'hot' and for that reason dispatched quickly by auction every evening. If an item was stolen from your shop, the chances were that you would find it in the mnada by evening. You could even send your servant to buy it back.

But Aloo convinced us that most items there were not stolen: the police came regularly to check. And if you knew the vendors there personally, if you befriended them, you could get just the selections you needed. The right sizes and the proper colours. He had started visiting the mnada regularly, on his way to check our box at the post office, and gave enticing reports of the cheap items on sale there. Finally he was given permission to buy, but only what was necessary and he started bringing home the stuff.

The question whether the goods were stolen was easily laid aside and for a few weeks the quality of life at home improved appreciably. Precisely those things we could not afford to have – whose absence betrayed our modest status, try as hard as we might to hide it – we could now get cheaply. At half the price or less. Mother, who worked alone in the store all day to make ends meet, did not have the heart to deny us these luxuries, these gifts that practically begged to be received. It was as if a rich uncle had unexpectedly turned up in town.

Aloo and I were soon newly outfitted for the coming Eid festival. Eid was always anticipated with great excitement all over town. In the few weeks preceding it, right up to the eve of the great day, shops stayed open late to make the most of the joyous season, while sewing machines hummed feverishly in their interiors and outside as bleary-eyed tailors worked overtime for anxious customers. But that season my brother and I were into ready-made importeds. The mnada gave us crisp white nylon shirts, made in Japan, and black ties to wear with them. The shirts had stiff collars and cuffs, and black plastic cufflinks. Next came leather shoes, with studs and steel inserts in their soles. Stretchable, nylon socks, which were new just then, followed.

Some weeks later, with the Eid behind us and business back in the doldrums, and school charging full steam ahead, came another treat – this time a potent relief which we had long awaited and fought for. It was our release from the irksome stiffness of our school shirts which, at Mother's orders, were sewn in our shop once a year from thick white drill to last through to the following year with continuous wear. How much we resisted wearing these dreadful garments which when new stood out like the starched khaki of the police! They gave us the dubious distinction in school of being the only two boys in drill. But wear them we had to and Mehroon, my sister, even had our initials sewn in black on the tails to keep us from squabbling first thing in the morning. These shirts saw their remaining days on the playing fields and in the streets. They were replaced by new, ready-made ones of soft cotton called 'Fuji'.

Aloo brought chocolates and orangeade, 'Oxford' compass boxes and 'Baby' pens. Straw schoolbags were abandoned for satchels made of plastic. The girls did not prosper as much as we did. Their clothes could only be sewn at home or at a dressmaker's from material bought downtown. Such speciality items the mnada appeared not to have. Once, though, Mehroon got some bras when she enquired of him about a particular brand. He was the expert. He could tell us what could be afforded and what had to be done without. And like a father in our fatherless household he brought home the goodies. He went alone on these trips; I never accompanied him, feeling shy and too embarrassed to venture into the bustling mnada to shop for the home.

We used to walk to school, the two of us: along two long streets, a walk of about three miles. First came Livingstone Street, a dirt road passing mainly through an African neighbourhood, then the paved United Nations Road that passed through a Hindu then a mixed rich locality. Near the end of Livingstone Street we would pick our friend Meghji up – which meant waiting impatiently at the door for him while he got dressed or had his breakfast. They were a poor family, their store a long narrow booth at the front of their house, flush with the street. There his father sat as we arrived, dispensing kerosene and matches and sugar and muttering from time to time, 'Oh God, make me good!' His mother was very fair and fat.

'Aloo is sick!' she observed one day when I arrived alone.

'Yes, Auntie,' I said, 'he stepped on a nail.'

46

The Relief from Drill

She saw us off as usual from the doorway, hands on her hips, the flesh on her fat arms loose and dangling at the sleeves.

We had walked past the crossroads, having observed from a distance the clock in the fire station office and decided to quicken our pace, when in his inimitable way Meghji made the revelation.

'Your mother surely gives Aloo a lot of money to keep, bana. He walks like a rich man! A whole wad of dough – he should not show it around.'

Perhaps his mother had asked him to say this. My heart sank. The doubt that had lurked in my mind like a thin mist whose presence I could barely sense now became concrete and dark and precipitate. I did not say much and we continued on our way, he telling bawdy jokes and I listening.

That afternoon I told Mother. Her face tightened, becoming white in a gesture we had learnt to recognise as more of sadness than of anger. Mehroon was also there in the store. She was Mother's chief lieutenant and self-styled executor. Often, a tyrant. The news gave her a particular thrill.

'Salah!' she exclaimed. 'How dare he cheat us!'

And her mind went through all the schemes he could have used to pilfer the cash. She did not hit upon the truth just then. Nothing was said for the next few days about the matter. Mother was noticeably quiet waiting for Aloo's next move. But neither he nor Razia nor Firoz suspected anything was amiss or the reckoning that lay ahead.

A few afternoons later, Aloo said he would go to the mnada. First he went upstairs to the flat for a bath. Mehroon's eyes lit up. She looked at Mother who was behind the counter near the cash box. Ten minutes later, as she timed it, Mehroon took the spare bunch of keys from Mother and followed Aloo upstairs. What happened there we heard from her. She opened the door and went in. The bathroom was to her left, and he wasn't in it. But she knew

47

exactly where he was. She went to the sitting room which also served as Mother's bedroom. It ended on one side in a wedge-shaped corner against which was placed a huge wooden closet that closed off a small triangular area at the back. At the back of the closet, in a small access between the bottom and the floor, Mother kept some cash: for emergencies and long-term debts. To get to the cash you had first to climb up over the six-foot closet, crouch under the ceiling and jump down into the small area behind. You had to be small which meant only Aloo and I could be used for the task. In that small area Mehroon found him. How she got him to come out she did not tell us, but we could guess. Her word was command.

She came downstairs triumphantly, holding him by the hand, and took him towards Mother. All the while he looked down, and I could feel his cheeks burning with the shame.

'Ask him what he was doing!' Mehroon proclaimed to us, releasing him with a shove.

That night while the rest of us sat in the sitting room around the radio talking in low tones to ourselves, Mother got up abruptly and went to the other room where with lights off he was in bed, hoping perhaps to fall asleep before the inevitable. He had gone through much during the rest of the afternoon and at dinner – Mehroon's taunts and questioning as she extracted from him all the accounts of his purchases and the details of his exploits that had now come to an end.

It turned out that he had bought most of the things downtown at regular prices. The mnada he had used mainly to quote cheap prices. The difference between what he quoted and what he actually paid he had made up by taking from the savings behind the closet, which were almost all used up.

My heart contracted and I grieved silently as I heard Mother say something in a heavy voice in the next room; and after that:

The Relief from Drill

'Will you do it again?' twice in succession. Then the sound of smacks as she slapped him on the thighs with a leather slipper, and his wailing reply, 'No, no.'

She returned to the sitting room, her face white, her lips pressed.

The Driver

He parked the stationwagon outside the goldsmith's shop and a bunch of schoolboys in rumpled, soiled uniforms of white and grey tumbled out of it from all sides. He watched them take off in all four directions for their homes. Then he carefully wiped the oil from their hair off the seats, locked the car doors and sauntered towards Nurmohamed's store across the street.

A bicycle speedily crossed his path and came to a wobbling stop a short distance away at the intersection. On the main road, the daily bread cart came creaking into sight, a fellow pushing it from behind and another pulling it. Now it pulled up at the intersection and waited. It was four o'clock in the afternoon and humid after the rains. As he walked he put his hand behind his neck and softly rubbed the sweaty skin there. Wet globules of dirt formed under his fingers. The inside of his shirt collar felt wet to his touch and he cursed at the heat.

Nurmohamed, who had followed his arrival from inside the store, now watched him cross the street. He sat, in a white singlet and a worn, green loincloth, perched on a carseat atop a wooden crate. Through the two storefronts he looked out on the two streets. He was surrounded by his wares, sitting practically in their midst. Crates heaped with grain and spices formed an uneven chequerboard displayed to the main street on one side; a wood-topped counter with a fly-specked glass front containing old yellowing items closed off most of the other side, leaving a small

50

passageway behind him. Tufts of grey hair jutted out from under his soft fat arms. His uncovered chest was a jungle of grey hair, his layered chin had a white stubble, and his white head was cropped close. His hands were in continuous motion. He would put a handful of spice or gum on a piece of square paper, then fold it rapidly, twice, to make a cone, then a third time, and finally tuck the remaining edge in and throw the finished packet into a basket. It would fetch ten cents from his mainly African customers.

From where he sat he could reach and measure out grain for them with a rusty milk can attached to a long handle. And he could extend a small metal tray to collect their money and return change. An old wooden cash box stood on the table in front of him. He did not have to move. They called him Mzee Pipa – Old Barrel. He was known far and wide, Mzee Pipa, the fat Indian shopkeeper of Kichwele Street, who would gyp you of a penny if he could. His weak legs could not carry his weight, and he had to be supported by the driver when he walked.

Inside the store was dark and cool. A large and dirty green tarpaulin sheet hanging from an awning protected the counter side from direct sunlight in the afternoons. Behind him were stacks of old British newspapers, *The Observer*, *The Illustrated London News*, *News of the World*, wrapping paper for sale to neighbouring stores. Behind the papers were gunny sacks filled with grain and behind these, in the storeroom, was complete darkness where no light, electric or sun, ever reached, and where only the servant ventured. There were cupboards on the walls that had not been opened for years. The place was infested with rats and cockroaches. An odour of spice and grain mixed with cockroach egg and wet gunny permeated the air inside.

The servant, a young boy who sat outside on the weighing scale under the awning, apparently with nothing to do at this hour, looked up as the driver approached.

'Eh, Idi,' spoke Nurmohamed in a hardly audible croak to the driver. 'Now take the food to the mosque.'

It was Friday today, the day of charity, when shopkeepers changed ten-cent coppers into pennies that servants then handed out to the scores of beggars expectantly touring the streets rattling their cans. On Fridays also, Nurmohamed fulfilled a family obligation and he sent his weekly offering to his mosque.

Idi walked towards the back of the building where a side door opened into the courtyard and the stairs. But first he passed it, turning into the open lot behind the building, covered with shrubs, trees and refuse, and stopped beside a pawpaw tree to urinate against the stained, yellow back wall. It was used by the servants throughout the day and the area was covered with a thick stench. He had to hold his breath.

He had used the toilet upstairs several times before, until he was caught emerging out of it once by Nurmohamed's wife and bawled out. So it was the wall for him, or one of the row of toilets in the mosque courtyard, where he could sneak in unseen. Wait, he had thought then, smarting from the insult. We'll have our day.

Upstairs the woman was taking her nap in the bedroom. The flat was quiet. All the curtains were drawn and it was cool. On the dining table, which was covered with a red and white checked plastic sheet, was a plate of food covered with a newspaper. Idi opened the pantry and brought out three hardened, stale chappatis and wrapped them in paper. He took the wrapped chappatis and the covered plate downstairs to the store and announced, 'I'm going.'

'Wait,' croaked the shopkeeper and from the cash box in front of him he took out a fifty-cent coin. 'Here, give this to her.' He started to cough, a deep, interminable wheeze.

The driver put the coin in his shirt pocket and crossed the street towards the car. The goldsmith was closing up. Near the goldsmith's was a butcher's also owned by Arabs. A smile lit up his face as he passed it. Early morning, every day, a truck came to deliver meat and the event almost always ended at the brink of bloodshed. At an innocuous seeming moment one of the African delivery boys would put a palm to his lips, blow a tremendous fart, and muttering 'Y'Allah!' like an Arab, pause for a moment. This was the cue. One of the younger butchers would come running out, brandishing a knife, an axe or a steel, swearing in Arabic. 'You son of a dog! Your father's arse!' Whereupon the other delivery boys, strategically placed and on the mark, joined in, provoking with taunts and musical farts, and were hotly pursued by the screaming Arabs right to their waiting truck. At some moments the excitement reached such a pitch that bystanders were tempted to join in the fun and sometimes did.

Idi had never succumbed to the temptation. It did not suit his image. He was a driver trained by another driver at the District Commissioner's office in his village and hoping for a government job. His khaki shirt and black trousers were of smart 'American' drill, and his black, leather shoes, although bought at a local auction, were polished. In contrast the delivery boys came barefoot and in tatters, hauling large hunks of bloody beef on their backs. No, he thought, as he reached the car, he was definitely not one of them.

He looked the car over and fondly stroked its warm and shiny roof. It was a light green Ford Taunus, three years old. He wiped it with a cloth every day. Nurmohamed had bought it to carry his son to school. He had then accepted to transport the neighbours' kids too, for a fee. This would pay for its upkeep. The son had died suddenly from an illness, but the transportation of kids continued.

Inside the car through the rearview mirror he could see Nurmohamed in his singlet on his high seat, hands still in motion. The man had always drawn from him feelings of disgust or pity. The personal attention he had to pay him was the worst part of his job. Fat and asthmatic, spluttering and coughing in his filthy store from morning till evening, he had to be assisted to walk, had to be lowered to his stool to take a wash. And with his small but sharp-tongued wife, harbouring a double grief. First the death of the son Amin who had come to them late in life after an unbroken line of seven daughters. Idi had been quite fond of the boy. At the funeral the woman, screaming and beating her breast, had to be restrained from running after the hearse. Idi and one of the daughters had held on to her while the hearse pulled away to the sound of wails. Later he had driven the mourning Nurmohamed and a few neighbours to the cemetery. Six months later their third daughter, wife to a drunkard, jumped to her death from the third floor of a building. What, he had often wondered, does tomorrow hold for these two? Do they feel a desire to walk out of their dark flat or their equally dark store and into the sun and breathe the fresh air, free from the smell of gunny and DDT and stale turmeric? Their future buried with their son, they continued now with what they had always done but with no purpose, no end in sight. The two-storey building named after him, Amin Mansion, was like a mausoleum over them.

There were stories of how he had made his money in the shack that used to be where Amin Mansion now stood. Once the police had raided it, looking for stolen jewellery. And Nurmohamed had taken them around by the light of a kerosene lamp that all the while contained the jewels. It was an Indian inspector of police, no less, who had been thus fooled. Then at another time he had swallowed a numbered hundred-shilling note so as not to be caught in possession of it.

Idi eased the car into reverse and backed out into the street. Then he drove forward and turned right into Kichwele Street. He cruised behind a bus for a while before it entered a stop lane and he passed it. A rally to support independence was in progress at the Mnazi Moja grounds where from the back of a pickup truck a man

The Driver

in shirt sleeves, a schoolteacher, was addressing a small crowd with a small megaphone. Soon he reached the mosque and drove into the compound which spanned a full block and parked behind another car.

He got out with his two packages. In deference to their common God, Nurmohamed's and his, he held the covered plate of fresh food in his right hand. Diagonally across from him where he stood beside the car, near the gate through which he had just driven in sat two women on the pavement with white enamel begging bowls in front of them. Their heads were covered. Behind them was an arched doorway that led into apartments for old women without means. One of the two was much older than the other, her face was pale pink, her hair white-golden, and her body frail. She was eating rice from her bowl, applying a fistful onto her wet old mouth and then rubbing the remainder off against the lip of the bowl, humming all the while. A tireless fly kept buzzing about her hand, weaving circles between the bowl and the ancient face. The other woman, darker and stronger, stared fixedly in front of her and did not stir as he approached. She was Nurmohamed's sister.

The driver approached her with some misgiving, as always, for she had nothing but taunts or complaints for him. She seemed to hold him responsible for her brother.

She looked up and grumbled. 'Why are you late? I have not eaten all day, do you know that? Does your master know that? Who cares if an old woman starves, if she's sick, if she's dying . . . ? Did you tell him not to come to my funeral? Tell him not to lay a foot there . . . not to come to my funeral. I have let it be known . . . he won't be allowed. Let him regret it forever. For what past sins we suffer . . . no sons, no husband, and a brother worse than not having one . . . ay, you heard me, tell him! In these arms I rocked him. Now he doesn't know me . . . I have no one in this world, nobody loves me. It's that witch, I tell you . . .'

'But God loves you,' the driver said to humour her. He bent

forward to hand her the package in his left hand and his eyes twinkled in amusement.

'What do you know?' she taunted in return. 'Are you His messenger or something . . . does He whisper things in your ears . . . ?'

As she said this he hesitated, felt the weight pulling down on the right hand as if to beckon. Then on impulse he reached out this hand pulling back the other and gently placed the mosque food, God's share, in front of her beside the bowl. The half-shilling clinked into the empty bowl when he dropped it and he stood up. He felt strangely elated.

She pushed the newspaper wrapping aside where it fluttered a little from a gust and when she saw the contents, sweet and fragrant yellow rice and curry still warm on the plate, she gave a chuckle and poured the curry on the rice. He left her and walked to the window where they received food for the mosque and handed over the second package. The boy at the counter unwrapped it, checked the contents – three dry chappatis – and scribbled a chit in Gujarati for him to take back.

As he crossed the compound on his way to the car, Idi let the note flutter away from his hand. His days with Nurmohamed would soon be over.

English Lessons

At a few minutes past eight, as always, Mr Stuart strode into the classroom gripping his cane. Conversations broke in midsentence, yells got stifled, and chairs rocking on hind legs landed firmly on all fours. A few stray characters quietly slipped back into their chairs and the remaining titters and murmurs from the less controllable quarters in the back rows finally petered out. It was as if a noisy radio had been abruptly switched off, leaving only the memory of its sound to sully the stillness.

Stuart, as he was called, appraised the scene for a moment, standing at his table, and then went back to the door to close it. He was tall and bony and walked with a little stoop. He was assistant headmaster, responsible for discharging the mandatory punishment on the backsides of latecomers: as a result of which he always came a few minutes late, to an uproarious class revelling in its short freedom.

As the door swung to a close, Rafael came thumping down the corridor, basket bobbing in hand.

'Sorry, Sir,' he said, panting, as the door swung open again. His black face was streaming with sweat and his clean white shirt disarrayed. He was barefoot.

'Bend-bend-bend,' said the master in a bored voice and delivered two cursory smacks on the proffered khaki bottom.

At this point Rafael goofed. He could have walked to his seat nursing his bottom. Instead he proceeded to remove from his basket a pair of polished black shoes which he dropped on the floor with a clatter.

An impish smile came over the stern, old face.

'What now, Rafael! Shoes in the bag!' He moved closer to look, peering as if at a specimen. 'Straight from the comics, this,' he called out over his shoulder.

'Send it to *Readers' Digest*, Sir!' called out a voice.

Stuart turned around with a snarl. It was the same voice that had called out 'Holy Ghost!' a few days ago; the owner of which sat fidgeting with a pencil, looking down at his desk in mock innocence. Stuart turned to the problem at hand.

'Well, now . . .'

Rafael was the only black boy in the class, always neat, a little timid.

'I was running, Sir,' he was explaining in earnest, '. . . and there's a lot of mud on the way . . .'

'Shoes are meant to be worn, Rafael, to keep our feet clean,' began Stuart unctuously, enjoying himself. 'Look at you – clean shoes and muddy feet. Will you slip on these glittering objects now – or do you propose to present us with the spectacle of your muddy paws all day long?'

Laughter. In Stuart's class laughter was a prolonged and exaggerated affair: anything to keep the old codger going and postpone the impending lesson.

'It was raining last night . . .'

'You boys have to be taught even the rudiments of manners, the rudiments of hygiene. Haven't you seen the mamas sitting all day outside the hospital – with kids with worms in their feet, worms in their bellies? Just to be able to show your new shoes at the Girls' School . . .'

Howls of delight at the magic words. A planted joke.

'And in the rain, you'll go around naked to save your

58

clothes . . .' He started muttering under his breath, the dark scowl returned to his face.

It was not known in class where Stuart originally came from. He looked neither European nor Asian. He sounded English, but not quite. The conclusion was that he was a Eurasian, perhaps even a camouflaged Goan. He always came in a cream or a light brown suit, wore a hat and carried a briefcase. The face was of a skeleton, a thin, pale skin stretching across it, his teeth rarely showing even when he laughed. It gave his scowl a distinctive ferocity and earned him the nickname Frankenstein. It was in fact one of the most feared faces in school. His lower lip jutted out and moved continuously during his silent mutterings. The boys never knew if those were real words he muttered or if he just pretended. But when he did that for what seemed like an eternity you felt your entire ancestry held up to ridicule and dismissed with contempt. 'Right up to Adam!' as Kanji said. Kanji, of whom Stuart said, 'Born in the gutter, bred in the gutter.'

The latecomer hugging his seat, the lesson started. The final chapter of an abridged *Tom Brown's Schooldays*.

'It was the summer of 1842 . . .' Stuart began. He preferred his own reading to the boys' imprecise intonations. 'Wot-wot-wot' he would sometimes yell in derision at an ill-pronounced question. This time he did not proceed beyond 1842 in his reading. The year brought memories and he digressed. And the boys prayed he would keep on digressing until the bell rang. The class was quiet and attentive and responded positively to his humour.

. . . The England of 1842. Young England, of rolling hills, lush forests, and stately homes. Where character was taught in schools . . . honour and courage were not mere words . . . and don't think sportsman's spirit was confined to the cricket pitch (a nod toward the door), you numbskulls, who use the pitch as a market for haggling and for community vendettas. (A titter: the barb goes home.) England, an island on the map, a beacon for the world . . . The summer of 1842 . . . from Rugby to college – perhaps Balliol, or Jesus – and then into the world to help a fresh breed of boys grow into men . . .

'Where is Balliol?' he asked suddenly. A question he would have answered himself, but for half a dozen hands in the air now, wagging fiercely. The closest hand in the second row was acknowledged, and Lalji shot up from his chair.

'Balliol is the college of Oxford!' All in one breath, hoarsely. 'I mean, Sir . . .'

Interrupted by a jeering howl from the master and the class held its sides. It was going to be a great day.

'Do you have to bark out your answer, man?' Red-faced, Lalji sat down, and faced his grinning neighbour. 'Show some grace, some poise.' And then, with a trace of regret, perhaps, at seeing the demolished face looking back at him in a daze: 'I know, your voice is breaking . . . but some grace, some poise, man . . . stand up first, compose yourself, and speak up, "Balliol is a college at Oxford." ' And then the mutter once more: pedigrees in question.

Stuart's mission in school was to civilise. Two months before, the class had been instructed on the use of the 'English-style' toilets. This, after he discovered a 'mess' on the lavatory floor. 'Do you think the bowl is there to wash your faces in, you numbskulls?' And then, grinning like a mischievous dog, he revealed a happy discovery: 'And tell your other teachers the seat is not to be mounted either!' The 'other teachers' were Indians. The boys wondered how he had found out who squatted on the toilet seats and who didn't – perhaps he went around peeping under the partitions in the staffroom lavatories?

Half way through the class Fletcher came to read an announcement. Fletcher was one of the new expatriate teachers from England, scruffy and eccentric, for whom Stuart showed a marked distaste. He was in charge of the Drama Society, which was

60

currently producing *A Passage to India*. The class had heard his announcement before, which he read again from a crumpled piece of paper. He was looking for Chagpar, his lighting man – and was told, as he had been several times before, that Chagpar was in Form IB. This was Form IA. He left, a little flustered. He never seemed to find Chagpar. Stuart returned to his digression.

It was one of his last classes of the year. It also turned out to be one of the last he taught in the school. The boys of Form IA prided themselves in having got rid of him.

◇

For Stuart had a secret. There was a woman in his home. He lived in the Teachers' Quarters. But who was this woman? If she was his mother, it was argued, she would be well into her seventies and that would explain the mystery. But if she was his wife . . . well, there was no knowing old Stuart the lecher . . . all those mentions of the Girls' School. She could be anyone. A kept woman? That would explain the secret. Perhaps she's an ogre, someone said, a dahkun.

It was Sumar's idea to investigate. Sumar was bright (one of the three 'geniuses' in class) but awkward and gawky. He sweated from his palms and constantly sniffled. He was also serious and did not find much in Stuart's jokes. And Stuart had developed distaste for him, which he showed with an occasional sneer but otherwise he left him alone. During the celebrated lavatory incident he picked Sumar for the demonstration. Poor Sumar had to endure all the stares and grins and back-handed remarks of his classmates as he crouched, squatted, and sat on the toilet seat at Stuart's bidding, looking very much like an embattled owl.

Kanji and Sumar were in the lead, followed by Rajani and Solanki, then Lalji and Rafael, returning from school in the mid-morning blaze. They entered a grove thick with coconut and mango trees. The ground under them crackled with fallen leaves as they walked, and the sky was completely hidden from sight. The

61

path went behind the Girls' School, which was still in session. In the Boys' School exams were over and school had ended abruptly to allow the staff to meet.

They emerged from the grove onto a hilly path. Before them, on the hill, rose the Teachers' Quarters: four brown concrete buildings enclosed by a tall wire fence. They started climbing up in a file of two. To their right was the ancient Shivaji Hospital, closed off by a wire fence and a densely packed hedge, from which peeped out shrubs of wild 'European tamarind,' so called because of its white flesh and mild taste.

'What time do you think it is?' asked Lalji from behind, a little anxiously.

Kanji took a peek at the sun. 'Wait,' he said. He did the clock trick. He picked up a stick, broke it in two, and flung the shorter part away. With the other he drew a clock face on the ground and planted it upright at the centre. The squat, twisted shadow pointed uncertainly toward the noon hour.

'It's eleven-thirty,' pronounced Kanji, looking up from the ground. He was not believed, but they started walking faster. Stuart would be expected for lunch.

At the open gate sat the watchman.

'Jambo, askari,' they said. 'Where does Mr Stuart live?'

'The third building. Third floor, number six. You are his pupils?'

'Yes, askari!'

Rafael said he would remain at the gate. Rajani stayed with him. The remaining four walked inside the gravelled compound. The buildings were well kept and looked new, each one had a bed of flowers at the side of its entrance. The walls were unmarked, the French windows painted white, and the floors and stairs polished red. There were a few people about. The boys took the stairs in single file in silence. When they reached number six, Kanji, with a glance towards the rest of them still climbing up, knocked twice on

62

the door. Sumar came to stand beside him and the other two stood behind.

The door opened a crack, and a black ayah peeped out.

'Is that his wife?' someone whispered at the back.

'His mother,' said Lalji, and tittered.

'Yes?' said the woman, her voice rising. Her face was round and fat, her eyes large and yellow. When she opened the door, the rest of her was big and wide and blocked the view in front of them. On one side of her was the kitchen door and on the other a window.

A faint sound came from behind her: a child's voice, a spoon scraping.

'We want to see the mama of the house,' said Kanji, a little hesitantly, as if asking permission. The others were silent, behind him.

The ayah heaved and stepped sideways in one motion, a block partition yielding, and they saw her, the second woman, at the head of the long table slurping at her tea, playing with her spoon. She looked young and old. Her face was smooth and pink, her hands delicate and small; her hair was long and dishevelled and fell in grey and white streams around her face to the table and the cup and saucer. Her front teeth were missing.

'Wha' you wan'?' she said. It was the voice of a crone. 'Professor . . . he gone . . .' Then she broke into a language none of them understood.

Lalji let out an involuntary grunt, like a muffled sob; then he forced a brief and nervous giggle. Kanji, in front of him, took a deep breath and stepped back, pushing them all out, and closed the door behind him.

The next morning Stuart strode into class as usual. There were no more formal lessons these last days of the year and the affairs of the school were finally winding down amidst rising excitement and impatience. The mood infected one and all. There was even a trace of levity on the usually scowling face, but the quiet that

63

confronted him caught him by surprise and he looked up as he went to the blackboard to place the cane on the chalk tray.

There was something taped on the blackboard which drew his notice mid-stride. It brought his head up with a jerk. It was the cover from a paperback edition of *She*. It showed in garish colours an ogre-like woman. Under it someone had scribbled in chalk: 'SHE WHO MUST BE LOVED!' Beneath that someone else had added for extra effect: 'Frankenstein's monster!' in a strangely uneven hand.

Stuart turned slowly to face them: behind the sternness this time traces of his pain.

The Sounds of the Night

Yes, I would say for many weeks after, I have seen Satan. I have seen the face of Azazil. And at what other time than the quiet stillness of that deepest point of night, at four, when the spirits take dominion and most men sleep; only a few hardy souls venture out to seek the eternal. At that hour there are no cars on the road, no bicycles. The breeze has not started to blow and the air feels dull and spent . . . and the street lamps let out a glow that hangs suspended in a haze that never quite makes it to the ground. Into this quiet an occasional sound of feet would wander in and as quickly wander out.

I was eight years old then. I would sit on our second-storey windowsill looking down at the street, knees and forehead pressed against the cool iron bars, half curtain pulled aside on its slack spring, awaiting this occasional wanderer. Often only the sound of footsteps came in rapid clip-clops, with no person in sight as whoever it was walked otherwise silently among the shadows, anonymity preserved. And when I did see someone, it would be all of a sudden; my head would come up with a jerk, my eyes strained wide to check my wakefulness. The person who appeared in my sight would walk rapidly by and disappear, and the clip-clop sounds would gradually diminish to a point beyond which there was no certainty. At that hour they were autonomous and sourceless, these sounds, diffuse, coming from directions where

65

nothing moving was in sight: as though descended from above to announce the visitor and ascending in steps back into the heavens.

And when those sounds of footfalls on the tarmac ceased, when it seemed that the quiet would now last unpunctuated till dawn, there would come this lone mysterious cry: 'Salaa! Salaa!' A distant sound yet clear, rendered into the sky; not loud enough to disturb sleep yet with an acuteness that could stir one listening to the dark. A call to prayer, itself a prayer. From my perch on the window I saw no one on the main street below. But I pictured a tall, black man in a long white kanzu and white kofia, strolling up and down his small dark street with a tasbih in one hand. And calling out. A lone African mystic, a great soul. His cry periodic in strength, as he approached and receded along a parallel road. Then it ceased altogether, and complete silence returned; only to be broken in less than an hour by the sounds of the first bus of the day trundling along, announcing the dawn.

When I finally set eyes on him, he was as I had imagined him, the African mystic. In robe and cap, a tasbih in one hand, tall and distinguished. He was sitting sideways on the ground outside the open door of a local mosque – a whitewashed building of baked earth – playing bao by himself. I had wandered into this sidestreet in my haste to get to the mosque. Not his but ours. It was grey dusk, grim Maghrab, the time for evening prayer, not for straying into strange, dark places. Mysterious things could happen at this hour, spirits would be at large from some of these local African mosques which harboured old graves in their compounds. Yet I had stopped hardly two feet away from the man and stood there mesmerised. He would pick up all the stones from a hole and in a single movement across the game board drop them one by one in the succeeding holes.

He glanced up and I caught his look, deep and searching. I was in the presence of a great soul whom I felt I knew, I who had heard him from my window and followed his call in the night. And I waited for him to speak to me as I knew he must, even though he'd dropped his eyes back to the board. I thought I must tell this great soul that I knew him, I had heard him when he called out to God and His people.

'Where are you going to, child?' he said.

'To the mosque.'

'The Indian mosque. What do you do there?'

'We pray.'

'You don't pray, you make fun!' He started mocking. 'Ai-yai-yai-nyai,' he sang in a high-pitched voice.

Partisanship got the better of me and in a rage I cried, 'We don't make fun! We pray! It is *you* who makes fun!'

All this in one breath at the end of which I unclenched my fists, realising what I had done. I had offended the great soul. The look on his face had changed from startle to an acid severity. I was afraid and I stood fixed as if awaiting my punishment, a curse to fly out from his angry lips. He was still working his lips as I turned my back on him and ran.

'Watch whom you're talking to, child!' he called bitterly after me.

I ran as if the devil were after me, jumping over ditches and stumbling over stones before finally reaching the sanctuary of our mosque. I was in a sweat, flushed, and gasping loudly for breath. My socks and shoes were filled with sand and my legs were covered with dust. The caretaker seated me on a bench, gave me a glass of water and when I was rested told me to wash my legs and feet and go in.

◇

In a few months that incident was far behind me. Or so it appeared. No longer was I getting up at four to await the dawn with my temple pressed against the cool iron bars of our windows. It had taken time and a family effort, before I was able to sleep through the African's calls to prayer. I had convinced myself that he had fallen in my esteem. He had mocked and been arrogant. And the realisation dawned on me that he had been playing bao at the time of evening prayer! What kind of great soul would do that? He was, I concluded with some assistance, an ordinary mortal, perhaps more sinful than most.

It was a few weeks before final examinations in school and the panic and suspense that always accompanied this period had begun to set in. My brother Firoz, always the one for last resorts, decided that year to join the early morning worshippers for whatever benefit he could gain. Firoz was eleven then, three years my elder. Boys did not usually go to morning mosque without an adult, but Firoz was always the independent type. And he certainly needed all the help he could get in passing his exams, as Mother well knew. She gave him permission to go, provided he take someone along, and he asked me if I wanted to join him. I said yes hastily, before the offer could be withdrawn, and the matter was sealed. Mother gave me a brief look but said nothing.

Except for the first morning – when in my excitement I could not get to sleep the previous night and consequently could not get up and was almost left behind – everything worked according to plan. The alarm would go off on time and at a little after four the two of us would step out into the silent street. We were warmly dressed for the hour, he sporting an old blue blazer I was anxiously waiting to grow into, I a sweater. Our feet made the clip-clip-clopping sounds on the street that I had heard so often. Most of our way was lighted for we walked on Kichwele Street. We stayed in the middle of the road and kept up a spirited conversation in murmurs. Every few stores there would be the reassuring sight of a night watchman, fast asleep or grunting in his blanket or sitting awake chewing tobacco.

The only forbidding part of the journey was the walk through the Mnazi Moja grounds. During the day it was quite lively, and twice a year the Eid festival took place here, whose drums echoed far and wide; at its far end football was played every afternoon. But at this hour an oppressive and sinister darkness lay over it. The ground at our feet dropped off into blackness at every step, soft breezes like cold fingers of evil brushed past our cheeks. My heart would beat faster and I looked neither back nor sideways but straight at the lights in the distance, clutching my brother's warm hand as he looked out for stones or potholes. We did not talk and kept our sounds to a minimum until we were out of there and under streetlights once more. Then, with relief, we breathed easy and resumed conversation. The mosque was close by and there were people converging towards it, talking in low voices.

On the fifth morning, a few stores before the street entered the blackness two dogs leapt out at us from the shadows, growling with menace and blocking our path. No one in the area kept dogs. Watchmen were more convenient. My experience was that if you ignored a dog and walked on, it would bark at you but let you pass. And if that didn't work, it was said that you could pick up a fistful and threaten to throw it, or you could pull the dog's tail. Both were guaranteed to work. Dogs cowered when you picked up sand. But there was no sand on this main street and when I made a gesture of pretending to pick up some, one of my captors snapped at me and the other let out a fierce growl. These were no ordinary dogs. They were now on each side of me and I could feel the wet nose of one rubbing against my knee and the other sniffing my backside. They were large dogs and I was terrified, standing awkwardly in the middle of the street, not daring to make a false move lest a chunk of flesh be torn off my legs or buttocks. There was no watchman or pedestrian in sight.

As I squirmed and sobbed, each wet feel of a muzzle sending spasms through my body, in bits and pieces a story came to my mind, a story my friend Azim had once told me. In these same grounds at about this time of the night his father, who was very religious and never missed mosque, had seen a white dog. This dog had stayed ahead of him, stopping every few yards to look behind as if to beckon. But the dog was trotting away from the direction of the mosque. As soon as Azim's father realised this, he kept his eyes averted from the white form ahead and muttering prayers the rest of his way he had escaped.

One of the dogs blocking us was white, and I knew then for a certainty I was in the clutches of him, Azazil, the daitya Kalinga in one of his many guises to torment the faithful. The fallen angel, wise with the knowledge of thirty-six crore books yet evil because proud and arrogant. A great soul gone astray. And I had no doubt who had called him upon me: straining my neck for sight of a possible rescuer, I heard the distant cry – 'Salaa! Salaa!' The African himself had begun his rounds in the little street outside his mosque, he who had warned me at dusk one day. It seemed that evil forces were about to converge upon me. What would happen now? Would I be eaten alive, would my soul go to heaven or hell? Hopelessly I looked at my brother in terror, cringing from the two dogs, and began to wail with abandon.

Firoz had not suffered the ordeal as badly as I had. 'I will say the nandeali,' he said.

When this prayer is repeated seven times in succession with complete faith, your tribulations disappear. It is for use only in the direst of circumstances and I knew then of no circumstance more dire. I myself did not know the nandeali, too young as yet to call upon such forces. Before Firoz had quite finished – he was into the third time he told me later – a watchman appeared in his tatters, cleared his throat loudly, spat and swore angrily. Throwing chunks of torn rubber from a nearby tyre dump at the two dogs, he chased them away into the darkness whence they had come. Then with a blanket wrapped around his shoulders, he accompanied us to our destination.

Leaving

Kichwele Street was now Uhuru Street. My two sisters had completed school and got married and Mother missed them sometimes. Mehroon, after a succession of wooers, had settled for a former opening batsman of our school team and was in town. Razia was a wealthy housewife in Tanga, the coastal town north of Dar. Firoz dropped out in his last year at school, and everyone said that it was a wonder he had reached that far. He was assistant bookkeeper at Oriental Emporium, and brought home stationery sometimes.

Mother had placed her hopes on the youngest two of us, Aloo and me, and she didn't want us distracted by the chores that always needed doing around the store. One evening she secured for the last time the half a dozen assorted padlocks on the sturdy panelled doors and sold the store. This was exactly one week after the wedding party had driven off with a tearful Razia, leaving behind a distraught mother in the stirred-up dust of Uhuru Street.

We moved to the residential area of Upanga. After the bustle of Uhuru Street, our new neighbourhood seemed quiet. Instead of the racket of buses, bicycles and cars on the road, we now heard the croaking of frogs and the chirping of insects. Nights were haunting, lonely and desolate and took some getting used to. Upanga Road emptied after seven in the evening and the sidestreets became pitch dark, with no illumination. Much of the area was as yet uninhabited and behind the housing develop-

71

ments there were overgrown bushes, large, scary baobab trees, and mango and coconut groves.

Sometimes in the evenings, when Mother felt sad, Aloo and I would play two-three-five with her, a variation of whist for three people. I had entered the University by then and came back at weekends. Aloo was in his last year at school. He had turned out to be exceptionally bright in his studies – more so than we realised.

That year Mr Datoo, a former teacher from our school who was also a former student, returned from America for a visit. Mr Datoo had been a favourite with the boys. When he came he received a tumultuous welcome. For the next few days he toured the town like the Pied Piper followed by a horde of adulating students, one of whom was Aloo.

The exciting event inspired in Aloo the hope that not only might he be admitted to an American university, but he could also win a scholarship to go there. Throughout the rest of the year, therefore, he wrote to numerous universities, culling their names from books at the USIS, often simply at random or even only by the sounds of their names.

Mother's response to all these efforts was to humour him. She would smile. 'Your uncles in America will pay thousands of shillings just to send you to college,' she would say. Evidently she felt he was wasting his time, but he would never be able to say that he did not have all the support she could give him.

Responses to his enquiries started coming within weeks and a handful of them were guardedly encouraging. Gradually Aloo found out which were the better places, and which among them the truly famous. Soon a few catalogues arrived, all looking impressive. It seemed that the more involved he became with the application process, the more tantalising was the prospect of going to an American university. Even the famous places did not discourage him. He learnt of subjects he had never heard of before: genetics, cosmology, artificial intelligence: a whole universe was

72

out there waiting for him if only he could reach it. He was not sure if he could, if he was good enough. He suffered periods of intense hope and hopeless despair.

Of course, Aloo was entitled to a place at the local university. At the end of the year, when the selections were announced in the papers, his name was on the list. But some bureaucratic hand, probably also corrupt, dealt out a future prospect for him that came as a shock. He had applied to study medicine, he was given a place in agriculture. An agricultural officer in a rural district somewhere was not what he wanted to become however patriotic he felt. He had never left the city except to go to the national parks once on a school trip.

When Aloo received a letter from the California Institute of Technology offering him a place with a scholarship, he was stupefied at first. He read and reread the letter, not believing what it seemed to be saying, afraid that he might be reading something into it. He asked me to read it for him. When he was convinced there was no possibility of a mistake he became elated.

'The hell I'll do agriculture!' he grinned.

But first he had to contend with Mother.

Mother was incredulous. 'Go, go,' she said, 'don't you eat my head, don't tease me!'

'But it's true!' he protested. 'They're giving me a scholarship!'

We were at the table – the three of us – and had just poured tea from the thermos. Mother sitting across from me stared at her saucer for a while then she looked up.

'Is it true?' she asked me.

'Yes, it's true,' I said. 'All he needs is to take 400 dollars pocket money with him.'

'How many shillings would that make?' she asked.

'About three thousand.'

'And how are we going to raise this three thousand shillings?

Have you bought a lottery? And what about the ticket? Are they going to send you a ticket too?'

As she said this Aloo's prospects seemed to get dimmer. She was right, it was not a little money that he needed.

'Can't we raise a loan?' he asked. 'I'll work there. Yes, I'll work as a waiter. A waiter! – I know you can do it, I'll send the money back!'

'You may have uncles in America who would help you,' Mother told him, 'but no one here will.'

Aloo's shoulders sagged and he sat there toying with his cup, close to tears. Mother sat drinking from her saucer and frowning. The evening light came in from the window behind me and gave a glint to her spectacles. Finally she set her saucer down. She was angry.

'And why do you want to go away, so far from us? Is this what I raised you for – so you could leave me to go away to a foreign place? Won't you miss us, where you want to go? Do we mean so little to you? If something happens . . .'

Aloo was crying. A tear fell into his cup, his nose was running. 'So many kids go and return, and nothing happens to them . . . Why did you mislead me, then? Why did you let me apply if you didn't want me to go . . . why did you raise my hopes if only to dash them?' He had raised his voice to her, the first time I saw him do it, and he was shaking.

He did not bring up the question again and he prepared himself for the agricultural college, waiting for the term to begin. At home he would slump on the sofa putting away a novel a day.

If the unknown bureaucrat at the Ministry of Education had been less arbitrary, Aloo would not have been so broken and Mother would not have felt compelled to try and do something for him.

A few days later, on a Sunday morning, she looked up from her sewing machine and said to the two of us: 'Let's go and show this

74

letter to Mr Velji. He is experienced in these matters. Let's take his advice.'

Mr Velji was a former administrator of our school. He had a large egg-shaped head and a small compact body. With his large forehead and big black spectacles he looked the caricature of the archetypal wise man. He also had the bearing of one. The three of us were settled in his sitting-room chairs staring about us and waiting expectantly when he walked in stiffly, like a toy soldier, to welcome us.

'How are you, sister?' he said. 'What can I do for you?'

Aloo and I stood up respectfully as he sat down.

'We have come to you for advice . . .' Mother began.

'Speak, then,' he said jovially and sat back, joining his hands behind his head.

She began by giving him her history. She told him which family she was born in, which she had married into, how she had raised her kids when our father died. Common relations were discovered between our families. 'Now this one here,' she pointed at me, 'goes to university here, and *that* one wants to go to America. Show him the documents,' she commanded Aloo.

As if with an effort, Aloo pushed himself out of the sofa and slowly made his way to place the documents in Mr Velji's hands. Before he looked at them Mr Velji asked Aloo his result in the final exam.

At Aloo's answer, his eyes widened. 'Henh?' he said. 'All A's?'

'Yes,' replied Aloo, a little too meekly.

Mr Velji flipped the papers one by one, cursorily at first. Then he went over them more carefully. He looked at the long visa form with the carbon copies neatly bound behind the original; he read over the friendly letter from the Foreign Student Adviser; he was charmed by the letters of invitation from the fraternities. Finally he looked up, a little humbled.

75

'The boy is right,' he said. 'The university is good, and they are giving him a bursary. I congratulate you.'

'But what should I do?' asked Mother anxiously. 'What is your advice? Tell us what we should do.'

'Well,' said Mr Velji, 'it would be good for his education.' He raised his hand to clear his throat. Then he said, a little slowly: 'But if you send him, you will lose your son.

'It's a far place, America,' he concluded, wiping his hands briskly at the finished business. 'Now what will you have – tea? orange squash?'

His wife appeared magically to take orders.

'All the rich kids go every year and they are not lost,' muttered Aloo bitterly as we walked back home. Mother was silent.

That night she was at the sewing machine and Aloo was on the couch, reading. The radio was turned low and through the open front door a gentle breeze blew in to cool the sitting room. I was standing at the door. The banana tree and its offspring rustled outside, a car zoomed on the road, throwing shadows on neighbouring houses. A couple out for a stroll, murmuring, came into sight over the uneven hedge; groups of boys or girls chattered before dispersing for the night. The intermittent buzz of an electric motor escaped from Mother's sewing machine. It was a little darker where she sat at the other end of the room from us.

Presently she looked up and said a little nonchalantly, 'At least show me what this university looks like – bring that book, will you?'

Mother had never seen the catalogue. She had always dismissed it, had never shown the least bit of curiosity about the place Aloo wanted so badly to visit. Now the three of us crowded around the glossy pages, pausing at pictures of the neoclassic façades and domes, columns towering over humans, students rushing about in a dither of activity, classes held on lush lawns in ample shade. It all looked so awesome and yet inviting.

76

Leaving

'It's something, isn't it?' whispered Aloo, hardly able to hold back his excitement. 'They teach hundreds of courses there,' he said. 'They send rockets into space . . . to other worlds . . . to the moon –'

'If you go away to the moon, my son, what will become of me?' she said humorously, her eyes gleaming as she looked up at us.

Aloo went back to his book and Mother to her sewing.

A little later I looked up and saw Mother deep in thought, brooding, and as she often did at such times she was picking her chin absent-mindedly. It was, I think, the first time I saw her as a person and not only as our mother. I thought of what she must be going through in her mind, what she had gone through in bringing us up. She had been thirty-three when Father died, and she had refused several offers of marriage because they would all have entailed one thing: sending us all to the 'boarding' – the orphanage. Pictures of her before his death showed her smiling and in full bloom: plump but not excessively fat, hair puffed fashionably, wearing high heels and make-up. There was one picture, posed at a studio, which Father had had touched up and enhanced, which now hung beside his. In it she stood against a black background, holding a book stylishly, the nylon pachedi painted a light green, the folds falling gracefully down, the borders decorated with sequins. I had never seen her like that. All I had seen of her was the stern face getting sterner with time as the lines set permanently and the hair thinned, the body turned squat, the voice thickened.

I recalled how Aloo and I would take turns sleeping with her at night on her big bed; how she would squeeze me in her chubby arms, drawing me up closer to her breast until I could hardly breathe – and I would control myself and hope she would soon release me and let me breathe.

She looked at me looking at her and said, not to me, 'Promise me

. . . promise me that if I let you go, you will not marry a white woman.'

'Oh Mother, you know I won't!' said Aloo.

'And promise me that you will not smoke or drink.'

'You know I promise!' He was close to tears.

◇

Aloo's first letter came a week after he left, from London where he'd stopped over to see a former classmate. It flowed over with excitement. 'How can I describe it,' he wrote, 'the sight from the plane . . . mile upon mile of carefully tilled fields, the earth divided into neat green squares . . . even the mountains are clean and civilised. And London . . . Oh London! It seemed that it would never end . . . blocks and blocks of houses, squares, parks, monuments . . . could any city be larger? . . . How many of our Dar es Salaams would fit here, in this one gorgeous city . . . ?'

A bird flapping its wings: Mr Velji nodding wisely in his chair, Mother staring into the distance.

Breaking Loose

The rock band Iblis was playing. The lead guitarist and singer was a local heart-throb, a young Asian with fairly long hair and bell-bottom trousers now in the midst of another brisk number from the foreign pop charts. Close to the stage danced a group of modish, brightly dressed girls, proclaiming by their various excesses their closeness with the four band members.

Yasmin was at the far end of the dance floor with her girlfriends. Three of them occupied the table with the only chairs available, Yasmin and the other two stood around. Occasionally she would look up to take in the dance scene, the band, the modish girls, hoping to catch a vacated chair she could bring over. The band was loud, the room hot and stuffy, and the men were drenched with sweat and the girls fanning themselves with handkerchiefs or anything else they could find. A well-dressed black man, somewhat odd in a grey suit, his necktie rakishly loosened, emerged from the throng of dancing couples and went up to her requesting the dance. She went.

Of all the girls here, why me? I don't want to dance. I can't dance. From the centre of the dance floor where he'd taken her she threw a longing glance at her gang chatting away in the distance.

'I'm sorry,' he smiled, 'I took you away from your friends . . .'

'It's okay . . . only for a few minutes – ' she began and blushed, realising that unwittingly she'd agreed. After all it's an honour, she thought. He's a professor.

79

It was a dance that did not require closeness or touching – and she was grateful for that mercy.

'Daniel Akoto. That's my name.'

'I know . . . I'm Yasmin Rajan.'

It's all so unnecessary. I'm not the type. He should have tried one of those cheeky ones dancing barefoot. Now that would have drawn some fun.

She looked at her partner. He was graceful, much more – she was certain – than she.

She was a head shorter than him. Her long hair was combed back straight and supported with a red band, in the manner favoured by schoolgirls, and she wore a simple dress. This was the middle of her second year at the University.

'Good music,' he said.

'Yes, isn't it? I know the lead guitarist . . .'

'But too western, don't you think?'

'I don't know . . .'

She felt oppressed by the ordeal, and the heat, and the smoke, the vapours of sweat, beer and perfume. There was the little worry too – why had he picked her and would he pursue her. He was looking at her. He was offended by her attitude and going on about Asians.

'. . . truly colonised . . . mesmerised . . . more so than the African I dare say.'

She didn't reply, trying her best to give a semblance of grace to her movements – feeling guilty, wholly inadequate and terribly embarrassed.

Just when she thought the rest of the dance would proceed smoothly – the music was steady and there was a kind of lull in the noise level – the leader of the band let out a whoop from the stage. There were whoops of rejoinder, followed by renewed energy on the dance floor. Akoto shook his head, and Yasmin watched him with dread.

Breaking Loose

'Look at that. Beatniks. Simply aping the Europeans . . . not a gesture you'll find original. Your kinsmen, I presume?' she forced a smile. *I hope he doesn't raise a scene.*

'There are African bands too, you know,' she said.

'But the *beat*, my dear, the *music*. Now take that song. Rolling Stones. What do you call *Indian* in that . . . for instance?' he persisted. 'Perhaps I'm missing something.'

Oh why doesn't he stop, for God's sake.

'What do you mean we're colonised?' she said exasperated. 'Of course we have our own culture. Come to our functions and see. We have centuries-old traditions . . .'

She had stopped dancing and there were tears in her eyes. She felt trapped and under attack in the middle of the couple of hundred people twisting and shaking around her. She could feel curious eyes burning upon her, watching her embarrassment.

She left Akoto in the middle of the dance floor and walked stiffly to her friends.

The next day she waited for the axe to fall. A call to the Vice Chancellor's office, a reprimand for publicly insulting a distinguished professor, a visitor from another African country. Perhaps she would just be blacklisted: a rude Asian girl, who doesn't know her place.

During lunch in the refectory one of her friends pointed him out to her. He was standing at the door, throwing sweeping looks across the hall searching for someone. She drew a deep breath and waited. His eyes found her and he hurried forward between tables, pushing aside chairs, grinning, answering courtesies on the way with waves and shouts. When he arrived, a place was made for him at the table at which he sank comfortably, putting both his hands in front of him. He looked at her.

'About last night . . .' he began. The other girls picked up their trays and left.

81

She laughed. 'You pushed them out,' she said. 'They'll hate you for that.'

Where had she found her confidence? He was in a red T-shirt – expensive, she thought. He looked handsome – and harmless.

'But not for long, I hope,' he began. His grin widened as he looked at her. 'Again I've removed you from your friends – but this time I've come to apologise. I'm sorry about last night. I asked you for a dance and then played a tiresome little radical.'

'It's okay. I'm at fault too. You see . . .'

'I know, I know. An innocent Indian girl in a den of wolves. But tell me – surely you expect men to come and ask you to dance in such a situation?'

She smiled, a little embarrassed. 'Usually the presence of girlfriends is enough to deter men one doesn't know . . .'

'Trust a foreigner not to know the rules.' He smiled ruefully. 'You came to have a good time with your friends and I spoilt it for you. Honestly I'm sorry. Look: let me make up for it. I'll take you for a drink. How about that?'

'But I don't drink . . . alcohol, I mean.'

'Tut-tut! We'll find something for you.'

He should not, of course, have pressed. But, as he said, he didn't know the rules. That's what she told herself when she found that she had accepted his invitation without any qualms.

'I'll take you to The Matumbi,' he said when they met later that afternoon. The Matumbi was a teashop under a tree, half a mile from the campus. It had a thatched roof that only partly shaded it, and no walls. She went in hesitantly, feeling a little shy and out of place. But apparently Akoto was one of the regulars. He motioned to the owner who came up and wiped a sticky table for them, and then he pulled up a rickety chair for her, dusting it with a clean handkerchief.

'Are you hungry?' he asked.

'No. I will just have tea . . . perhaps a small cake . . .'

'Righto! Two teas, one cake and one sikisti!' he called out.

She raised an eyebrow when the sikisti arrived. It was an egg omelette between two inch-thick slices of bread.

'It's called sikisti because of its price. Sixty cents!'

She laughed.

'That's the truth, believe me!'

Akoto was a professor of sociology, on loan from the Government of Ghana.

'What is your major?' he asked her after some time. 'What subject are you taking?'

'Literature.'

'Literature?'

'Yes.' *Now he thinks we are all shopkeepers.*

'Tell me: any African writers?'

'Yes. Soyinka . . . Achebe . . .'

'Things fall apart . . .'

'The centre cannot hold.'

He laughed. 'Ngũgĩ? Palangyo? Omari?'

She shook her head. She hadn't heard of them.

'Local writers. Budding. You should read Omari. Nuru Omari. She writes about the Coast – your territory. *Wait for Me*: that's her first book. I could lend it to you if you want.'

'It's okay . . . I'll borrow it from the library.'

He looked astonished. 'But it will take time before the library acquires it!'

'I'll wait . . . I don't have much time right now.'

'All right.' He was miffed.

'Now that I have made up for my rudeness,' he said at last, seeing her a little restless, 'I hope – having apologised and so on – perhaps we can go.'

I am studying literature and I have no time to read the most recent books. She felt guilty.

◇

83

When she saw him again it was after several days and he did not appear to notice her. He's got my message, she thought. I am not interested. Why did I go to the teashop with him, then? . . . Because he's so different. What confidence, what grace . . . so civilised, such a gentleman! That's it! she thought. He said we Asians are so westernised . . . aping the Europeans . . . mesmerised . . . what about him? All that external polish: he was a proper English gentleman himself! She would tell him so!

'Dear Professor Akoto,' she wrote, 'I wanted to tell you something. I thought I should tell it to you before I forget it completely. You called us Asians colonised. We are mesmerised with the West, you said. Well, have you observed yourself carefully lately? All those European mannerisms, language, clothes – suits even in hot weather: you are so much the English gentleman yourself! Yours sincerely, Yasmin Rajan. P.S. Could I borrow Omari's *Wait for Me* from you after all? Thanx.' She slipped the note under his office door.

He repeated his previous performance at lunchtime the next day, edging out her friends from the table.

'Your point is well taken,' he said. 'Touché and so on. But I thought we had forgiven all that. Still, I don't quite agree with you. And the reason is this: I know my situation. I struggle. In any case . . . Let's not argue. Let me show you my library. You can borrow any book you like.'

'You have your own library?' she murmured.

When she saw it she was dazzled. Three walls were covered with books. She had never before seen so many books belonging to one person – in a sitting room, part of the furniture as it were.

'You've read all these books?' she asked.

'Well . . . I wouldn't . . .'

'I envy you. You must be so knowledgeable.'

'Let's not get carried away now.'

'Do you also write?'

'Yes. But nothing out yet.'

He had a theory about African literature. 'It is at present digging up the roots,' he said. And that's what he was trying to do. Dig. 'So you can understand my obsession with authenticity. Even my name is a burden, an imposition.'

At The Matumbi, where they went that evening, she had her first sikisti. She talked about her background.

'My father was a pawnbroker,' she said, 'but pawnshops are no longer allowed, so now he has a tailoring shop. Hardly a westernised background . . .'

He smiled. 'Aren't you ever going to forgive me?'

'Tell me, do you think pawnshops are exploitative?' she asked him.

. 'Well, they tempt the poor and they do charge awfully high interest.'

'Yes, but where else can the poor get loans? Would the banks give them? And as for the high interest – do you know the kind of things they bring to pawn off? Old watches, broken bicycles, clothes sometimes. We have three unclaimed antique gramophones at home that we can't sell.'

'Is that right? Can I look at them? I might buy one. I like old things that are out of fashion.'

'Sure you can.'

He played badminton with the Asian girls one day, bringing along a shy young man from Norway. It was at a time (though they did not tell him) when they usually went to the mosque. After the game there was a heated discussion about China. And they arranged to play the next time a little later in the evening.

One afternoon, as agreed previously, Yasmin took him to her father's shop to show him the antique gramophones. They went in his car and he dropped her off outside the shop and went to park.

When he entered the shop her father met him.

'Come in, Bwana. What can I get for you?'

He was a short thin man with green eyes, wearing a long white shirt over his striped pyjamas.

'I came with Yasmin,' Akoto explained in his broken Swahili.

'Yes? You want to buy something?'

'I came for a gramophone –'

'Ah, yes! The professor! Sit, sit.'

Akoto sat on the bench uncomfortably and waited, looking around inside the shop. The shelves lining the walls were filled with suiting, the glass showcases displayed shirts. Yasmin's father went about his work. The girl soon arrived from the back door carrying an old gramophone. Behind her was a servant carrying two, one on top of the other, and behind the servant followed a tall thin woman: Yasmin's mother. While her father showed Akoto the gramophone, Yasmin and her mother went back inside.

'How can you bring him here like this?' said her mother angrily. 'What will the neighbours think? And the servants? It's shameful!'

'But Mummy, he is a professor!'

'I don't care if he's a professor's father!'

When they went back to the store the purchase was completed, Akoto and her father were chatting amiably about politics. Akoto was grinning, carrying a gramophone in his arms. He looked enquiringly at her.

Outside the store a few boys and girls from the neighbourhood walked by, throwing quick curious glances inside at the guest.

'Yasmin will stay with us tonight,' said her mother a little too loudly from the back doorway where she stood. 'She'll come back tomorrow. But she won't miss her classes – I hope that is alright.'

'Don't worry, Mama. It's perfectly alright.'

It was more than a week before they met again, briefly, in a corridor.

'Where do you eat lunch these days? You're the perfect salesman,' he said in good humour. 'You sell me an old gramo-

86

phone and disappear. You afraid I'll return it?' She gave some excuse.

Later she returned the books she had borrowed from him and declined an invitation to The Matumbi.

The sight of Akoto in her shop that day had driven her mother into a fit. By the time he had left the shop hugging the gramophone she was raging with fury. 'There are no friendships with men – not with men we don't know . . .' She said to Yasmin.

'The world is not ready for it,' her father said quietly.

'You stay out of it!' screamed his wife. 'This is between us two.'

He remained quiet but stayed within hearing distance, measuring out cloth for his tailors. If Yasmin expected any understanding, or even a reasoned discussion with an adult, experienced voice, it was from her father. But ever since she could remember, she had been her mother's business. And her mother, she believed, hated her for this, for being a girl. Yasmin was not the only child, there were three brothers. But ever since she could remember her mother was always admonishing, chiding, warning her – as if believing her capable of the worst. Now it seemed that all the horrors she had imagined possible from her daughter – against her, against the name and dignity of the family – were on the verge of coming true.

'What do you know of him?' She had been uncontrollable, obsessive, had gone on and on until she was hoarse and breathless. 'With an Asian man, even if he's evil, you know what to expect. But with *him*?'

At the end of the day the girl felt as if her bones had been picked dry.

Yasmin did not go to the end-of-year dance on campus. From her friends she heard of the one notable event that took place there. Professor Akoto, after sitting at a table all alone for some time and apparently after a little too much to drink, had got into a brawl with Mr Sharp of the Boys' School, calling him a CIA agent. Then he'd staggered out.

◇

India was not just the past, or the community, or even the jealous Indian communities of Dar. India was a continent, a civilisation, a political entity in the world. Only recently it had emerged from a long struggle for independence.

During the holidays Yasmin discovered her world. She read avidly about India, quizzed her father about it. India came as a revelation. Here in Africa she was an Asian, an Indian. Yet she had been a stranger to even the most recent Indian history. All she had received from her people about India were ancient customs, unchanged for generations, remotely related to the world around her. At first her acknowledgement of her origins seemed to her a reaction against Akoto, the African; yet it seemed to be harking back to the authenticity he had been talking about. In a strange and diabolical way it seemed to be bringing her closer to the man, as if what she was discovering was at his bidding, as if she had to go and discuss her findings with him, answer his challenges.

The world seemed a smaller place when she went back to the University. Smaller but exciting; teeming with people struggling, fighting, loving: surviving. And she was one of those people. People, bound by their own histories and traditions, seemed to her like puppets tied to strings: but then a new mutant broke loose, an event occurred, and lives changed, the world changed. She was, she decided, a new mutant.

Yasmin's father collapsed with a heart attack under the weight of two bolts of suiting in his shop, one month after the University reopened. A servant was dispatched to fetch a doctor, who arrived an hour and a half later. By that time the former pawnbroker had died.

Daniel Akoto attended the funeral. He sat among the men, initially on the ground, trying to fold his legs, sweating profusely, pressed from all sides. A black face in a sea of patient brown Asian faces. He was not wearing a suit, just a very clean white shirt, but this time some of the other men were in jackets. A servant saw the discomfited man and placed a chair for him against the wall adjacent to the door. Now Akoto could see clearly across the room. The body was lying on a low table behind which two men sat on the floor administering the last rites to the dead. The widow sat beside the dead man, sobbing, comforted by her daughter, occasionally breaking into a wail and joined by other women. Mrs Rajan looked away from Akoto when their eyes first met. She moaned and started weeping. She saw him again through a film of tears, lost control and gave a loud wail.

'You!' she screamed, 'what are you doing here? What kind of man are you, who comes to take away my daughter even in my grief . . . Who asked you to come? Go away!' She wept.

Akoto, understanding only partly her speech but fully the intent, tried to smile apologetically at the men and women now turning to stare at him.

'Go!' said the distraught woman pointing a finger at the door beside him.

No one else said a word. Akoto stood up, gave a respectful bow towards the dead man and left.

A week later Yasmin knocked on his door late in the evening and caught him in.

'Come in,' he said, putting away his pipe.

'I've come to apologise about that day.'

'It's all right. A funeral is not exactly where people are at their best . . . perhaps they are more honest though.' He eyed her.

'You could have us arrested! You could . . .'

'Don't be silly! Take a hold of yourself. What do you think I am anyway – the secret police?'

'You must despise us,' she said more quietly. 'You are educated, learned . . . your government has loaned you to us . . . You are a great man . . .'

'No, I don't despise you. And don't call me great for God's sake.' She began to laugh, a little hysterically. They both laughed.

'And you, I respect you.' He spoke calmly. 'You are brave. You left that gang of girls that day at the dance and since then you've done it again and again. It takes courage, what you've done, trying to break away from tribalism – that's all it is ultimately . . . Even coming here like this. I realise that and I like you.'

'Well, I like you too!' she said, too quickly. There was a silence between them. 'You know, it's not going to be easy . . . with my father dead, this will be the greatest shock to my mother . . . it will kill her, it will . . .'

'Now, now.' He went up to her, put her wet face on his shirt. 'We'll have to do the best we can, won't we?'

What Good Times We Had

At two o' clock she sent the servant upstairs to the flat to wake Ramju up. He came down fifteen minutes later, still drowsy from his nap. She turned towards him a look of exasperation which melted ineffectually into one of concerned affection. What would become of him when she left, she wondered, this uncouth, uncultured fish barrel of a man, her brother?

'I have to go see that bank clerk,' she told him. 'I'll be back in an hour or two.'

She felt a pang of guilt as his eyes sought hers for an instant. There was no choice, she told herself, as she had already done a dozen times before. She had waited too long and perhaps it was already too late. She had to go, as the others had done: her several younger siblings, whom she had helped to bring up, had gone on to study and then had stayed. She had to go and try to remain there. If possible to send for Ramju. But he was a hopeless case. A good businessman here but completely inept and destabilised when confronted with a sentence in English. He could not even get a tourist visa to go abroad. Alone, how would he fare? He was so dependent on her she even had to remind him to shave. A bachelor now in his forties. They had tried so hard to get him a wife. First their mother and father and then she herself – looking around, enquiring, sending proposals. But invariably he picked the smart and pretty ones, who took one look at him and turned up their noses.

She took the car. On the way she wondered how she herself would fare, not many years younger than him and equally unmarriageable. If she wanted to remain abroad she had to get married then, she thought, one way or another. And if she did . . . what would become of him, this man who had run a duka, a small shop, all his life, who knew nothing else, had no family in the country? Would he die here a lonely old man with his shop?

There was a fair amount of traffic in people and cars outside the bank. She turned into the driveway and parked at a spot outside the main entrance. The building was new, erected a few years after Independence as the headquarters of the national bank after the foreign banks were nationalised. Its modern expansive structure, grey and concrete, rose up a few storeys high to preside over an array of white-washed colonial buildings spread out around it. Applications to buy foreign exchange to send money out of the country were considered here. There was a ruling now that airplane tickets for foreign travel could be bought only with the bank's permission, which was not easy to obtain.

Clutching her handbag under one arm she took the front steps to the main reception area, a petite figure with dark features and thin long wavy hair, often mistaken, much to her consternation, for an Arab or half-caste. The bank clerk was waiting for her in the hallway.

'Ah – you're late!'

'Yes, I had a little work to do. Do you have the ticket?' she said, a little breathless.

'Yes – but there's a small problem.' A round fleshy face, a big body, clumsy gait. In a dark grey Kaunda shirt. He did not at all look like a bank officer. 'I gave it to my brother for safekeeping; we have to go and pick it up from his house. A small drive . . .'

She was piqued. 'I'm not your chauffeur to drive you around! Do you want the money or not? You should have asked him to bring it. Pick it up tonight, then, and bring it to the store first thing in the morning.'

You had to be tough with them, otherwise they would walk all over you. Even the price he'd asked was far too high. But there was no alternative.

'Look, Mama, I've run a lot of risks for you. I risk my job even talking to you like this. The CID know what's going on. Now, do you want to go? Tomorrow is another day. This ticket is all stamped and waiting, if you want it.'

'Okay, okay. Where, now?'

'Take the road to the University. I'll show you . . .'

She strode towards the car; he followed. She got in, closed her door and unlocked his from the inside. They drove out past the iron gates.

She drove aggressively, hooting at pedestrians and cyclists impatiently as she deftly dodged potholes and passed other cars. They left the city limits behind them and sped along the coastal road northward. The ocean was to their right and occasionally appeared as a glimmer through clearings in the trees and shrubbery. He sat comfortably beside her, the thought of which irked her. Like a husband, or a boss, arm resting on window, stomach pushing out. Enjoying the cool sea breeze. The sooner this was over with the better, she thought. Another price to pay. Soon however there would be no more prices to pay. Not such prices. Life wasn't easy where she would soon be but it couldn't be so bad. There was a price for everything here. And after all that, there was no peace to be had even at night time for fear of robbers. They lived on the edge, not knowing if they would be pushed off the precipice the next day – or if the hand of providence would lift them up and transport them to safety.

'Soon you'll be in Canada, Mama. Will you stay there for good or will you be returning to us?'

'Oh, no – I will leave this land for good only if they take me by the hands and feet and throw me out,' she lied, repeating an oft-quoted line. 'It's not easy there, you know. What's wrong with this place anyway?'

'True, true – you speak the truth Mama! Some people will never be satisfied. But this land gives enough.'

'Besides, this is my country. I was born here, my father was born here. So was my mother.'

What times they had had here, she thought with bitterness. On this very road they used to go on picnics in open trucks, cauldrons brimming with Sunday's choicest, singing, playing, laughing at the breeze that would blow their hair and muffle their voices . . . Food was abundant, fruit almost free, servants plentiful . . . violence, real violence, unknown . . . Who had ever seen a gun? . . .

Gone, wiped clean. A dream had passed. And now even if she were to describe those times to someone who had not been there he wouldn't believe her. Sometimes she wondered if what her mind remembered could really have happened.

'Slow down,' he said, 'turn right, there at that road.'

The University towers rose up dimly in a haze like a mirage further ahead in front of them. She waited for the traffic to clear, then took the turn quickly and drove some distance along the access road which was a clearing in the bushes partly layered with sand. It led towards the beach, a picnic spot. She could see the roofs of huts in the distance, hidden behind trees, and drove with difficulty over the uneven terrain that was covered with muddy potholes and clumps of grass.

'*What* does your brother do here?' she said in exasperation as the car jolted violently several times and they bounced on their seats. 'Do you know what spare parts cost these days?' He did not answer. 'What you can get of them . . .' she added grimly, peering ahead.

When they drew closer she saw the huts were burnt down,

94

gutted with fire, the roofs just a bunch of sticks. There was no one in sight. She turned to look at him and recoiled with horror at the inane smile on his face, the gleam in his large, yellow eyes. The hatred she saw there she had never seen in a pair of human eyes before.

And she thought of all the black men she had presided over almost all her thirty-seven years with scorn. The houseboys, the tailors, the customers, the hawkers, who came with the dawn, subservient, and disappeared into the night. Who no more belonged to her community of men and women than the flies on the walls. She thought of the thief who had threatened her with a knife after she had caught him stealing, who had put the fear of death in her; the choras – boys – she had been taught to look out for in the streets, who would touch you if they could; the one proposal she had ever had in her life, and that from a former chief, which she had spurned in rage, grieving a whole week afterwards at the insult . . .

Was this revenge, or plain avarice?

They found the body three days later, naked and abused, hanging by the feet from a tree branch. Her head was in the dirt, and her black hair, now caked with dust, spread out from it in a circle.

Ebrahim and the Businessmen

The house stood on a wide lot in Upanga, well away from the congested developments up the road. It was new and fairly large, divided into four apartments, one for each of the Teja brothers, building contractors. There was an extensive garden in front, with rose and jasmine bushes in the centre, periwinkle scattered at the hedges along the sides, banana and pawpaw trees in a corner, and bougainvillaea at the wire fence in front. Four cars were parked in the gravelled driveway. The curtains were drawn in the front rooms, letting through a faint and enigmatic glow from the light inside. Against the shrilling of insects in the garden came the occasional distant-sounding ejaculation or child's cry. Parties were often held here but this was the first time Ebrahim Kanji had been invited – not for a social but for a business meeting.

He had parked his small Fiat on the main road under a street lamp. As his feet went crunching along the gravelled path, there was in Ebrahim a feeling of anger and bitterness mixed with curiosity and triumph. So now they need me, he said to himself, these petty bourgeoisie, dukawallahs: because their world threatens to crumble around them. The men he was going to see belonged to his father's generation, and his anger was directed at them for the way they had treated his father.

Nurali Kanji – Ebrahim's father – had been an intellectual: idealistic and impractical. In the 1940s he had incurred the wrath of the businessmen of his Indian community, for being one of the

96

group of young men that had distributed a pamphlet laying down a general charge of mismanagement of community funds, calling for an open accounting system and for the money to be spent on local social projects. Three young men were principally involved; all three were punished and lived thereafter on the fringes of the community. A gang of loyal youth accosted the youngest of the three and threw a bottle of acid at his face, scarring him for life. The other two escaped lightly and were simply beaten up. One afternoon when Nurali Kanji was returning home for lunch, having reached the narrow alley in which he lived, he found four big women veiled in black waiting for him. They were armed with brooms, sticks and rolling pins.

'Bastard!' they shrieked. 'Satan! Where's the bitch that bore you?'

Nurali Kanji took his punishment in terror and went home weeping. It became a community joke later that one of his assailants was in fact a disguised youth who had been there in case Nurali turned hostile and attacked the women.

Nurali Kanji never found a respectable job after that, could never raise the loan to open his bookstore. He would receive odd accounting or clerical assignments and be asked to draft petitions to the government or to assist with the community newsletter. His son Ebrahim received free education as charity. His wife sold samosas to support the family. Until the last days of his life he showed supreme contempt for the businessmen and harboured a resentment at their growing successes.

Ebrahim now knocked on the door of the Tejas, one of Dar's leading business families. After being peeped at through the spy hole he was received by their daughter.

'Why, Ebrahim! Come in. So nice to see you.'

'I've come to see the businessmen.'

'Big shot, eh?'

Ebrahim remembered the days when he walked barefoot, when

this girl would pass him in derision. Now he had a reputation with
the girls for his machismo and his daredevil ways. He was tall and
powerfully built. His hair was combed flat in the traditional way,
but this act of defiance, together with his moustache and black
fiery eyes, only served to enhance his reputation. He was shown
into the sitting room.

'Ah, Minister! Come in, come in, please!' Jaffer Teja greeted
him with typical exaggeration and escorted him in, seating him
prominently on a sofa. Teja was a middle-aged man with a
pockmarked face and, like many of the businessmen present, wore
a Kaunda suit.

'Our boy Ebrahim,' he announced exultantly, 'is with the Vice
President's Office. This is a proud moment for all of us.' He looked
up as if to offer thanks to God.

'What can I do for you, gentlemen?' Ebrahim asked, sipping the
tea that had been offered him and helping himself to a savoury
from the serving table that had been placed in front of him. They
are grovelling at my feet, he thought with satisfaction. If only
Father had lived to see this day.

'Ebrahim . . . Ebrahim . . .' Jaffer Teja, who was obviously the
spokesman of the group, began, shaking his head. He was sitting
in a chair close to Ebrahim and facing him. 'You know what has
befallen us, our people . . . all their life's savings . . . the savings of
their fathers . . .'

What Teja was referring to was the recent take-over of properties that were let out for rent in a socialisation move by the
government. Only the houses that were occupied by the owners
were exempt from the take-over.

'You know how they made their money . . . They came as
paupers, sold peanuts, popcorn, seeds . . . and little by little,
through hard work, morning and night, they earned and saved.
They did not put their money even in banks! They were too scared
to do so. All they dreamed of was a piece of land, to build

something on it, something they could call their own, the prize of their hard labour.

'This government has betrayed us. We put our trust in it . . .' He looked sadly at Ebrahim.

'But what can I do?' asked Ebrahim, waiting for the punch line.

'You have influence, Ebrahim . . . or should I call you Minister Sahib?' Teja smiled and the other businessmen smiled politely. Some took the opportunity to clear their throats.

'But I can't give you back what the government took from you!'

'No no no no no! . . . But there are ways, Ebrahim . . .'

'Ways there certainly are,' spoke someone from the side.

'What ways.' Ebrahim asked.

'Take Thobani here . . . we call him Raju . . . Raju has two houses, his brother Shamshu has none. One of the houses can be transferred to poor Shamshu.'

'And poor Shamshu pays Raju a handsome rent,' Ebrahim said.

'But it's their family wealth! That's not stealing.'

'Does Raju really have a brother?'

No one spoke a word.

Ebrahim got up. 'Gentlemen, you are asking me to betray a trust. I don't know what exactly it is that you want me to do but obviously it's illegal.'

' "Illegal" is only a word, Ebrahim,' said Alibhai Teja. He was the eldest of the brothers, obviously their leader, a man with an enormous belly and a pendulous chin. He was flanked on both sides by businessmen and the girl who had let Ebrahim in had come to sit on the armrest of his chair.

'Many people have genuine grievances. Do you think the government will listen?' He spoke with authority. 'And what about the civil servants . . . they do nothing without bribes. To whom can one go with legitimate complaints?'

Ebrahim left the meeting, Jaffer Teja accompanied him to the door.

'Raju has a genuine complaint, Ebrahim. Only listen to him – give him five minutes of your time. Let me bring him to your office.'

Ebrahim left without a word.

◇

Ebrahim Kanji had been a much disliked boy. He had been dirty, rowdy and a bully. In school he had always been placed in the stream reserved for the dullards. But he was bright. From his father he had absorbed a love of learning, of arguing and of asking pointed, pertinent questions. The fact that such questions came from a scoundrel offended his teachers the more. In his final years in school his rowdiness transformed itself into extrovertism; his outcast status from the community left him open to friendships outside it. He took part in debates and drama, he was elected an official of the Party Youth League. His final examination result was among the best in the school and he was selected by the government to study political economy at the University. This success owed not a little to the changing face of the school in those years when it was converted from a community school to a public high school.

He had always been a radical, and at the University he had been a founding member of SNAFU, Students for a New Africa (Union), a political organisation that was in general agreement with the government's policies. Its influence was such that when an argument arose between the University students and government over the military training of the students, its members were among those selected to meet with the President. Ebrahim Kanji was one of those.

Two days after his meeting with the businessmen, a little before lunchtime, Ebrahim looked up from his desk to see Jaffer Teja and Raju Thobani escorted into his office by a clerk. He was not surprised: he had not expected the businessmen to give up so easily. He wished, though not very strongly, that he had spurned their first approach. But the desire to see them grovelling had been too tempting.

Raju Thobani was a small mousy man whose distinguishing feature was his near baldness. He had obviously put himself under the patronage of the Tejas. Ebrahim indicated the two chairs across from him and the two men sat down respectfully and braced themselves to speak.

'Well,' said Ebrahim, having eyed them in turn and now looking at Jaffer Teja.

Jaffer Teja motioned to Raju. 'Tell him,' he said.

Raju began with an apology. 'Mr Kanji, you are a busy man, learned and distinguished . . . I am sorry for bringing you my troubles . . .'

'It's all right,' said Ebrahim.

'He agreed to listen,' said Teja, not quite accurately, and met Ebrahim's eye, as if willing to argue the point. 'Proceed,' he told Raju.

'Mr Kanji, it's like this,' said Raju, no longer hesitant. 'My father left all his property to me because I was the eldest in the family . . . you know how our families are traditionally . . . the eldest brother is the father . . . and he takes care of the rest of the family. So the two properties were put in my safekeeping for the family. Now does that mean my younger brother Shamshu should miss out because of that? My father worked hard for these properties . . . not that they are large buildings. Just two flats. Now one of them is taken away.'

'What can I do?' Ebrahim said. 'It's not in my hands. You have to go to the Ministry of Housing.'

'Just tell me,' pleaded Raju, 'simply tell me – is it fair my younger brother should be deprived?'

'You should file an appeal; there are procedures.'

'Ebrahim, you are laughing at us,' Jaffer Teja shook his head

101

sadly. 'The Ministry-wallahs won't listen but all it takes to remedy the situation is a small change in the deed.'

'What small change?'

'Well, the ownership of flat number 9 on 66 Ushariki Road is to R S Thobani: "S" for Samji their father. If we erase the "R" we will have "S Thobani": "S" for Shamshu. A small price for justice.'

'Small for you,' said Ebrahim in a dismissing tone. 'I'll make enquiries at the Ministry,' he said to a grateful Raju.

Jaffer Teja stayed behind as Raju left. 'My brothers and I will consider it a great favour if you help this poor man. He is hardly a capitalist exploiter as you clearly see.'

The next morning at coffee break Ebrahim strolled over to the Ministry of Housing and demanded the deeds for flat 9 at 66 Ushariki Road. He was handed the file deferentially and took it with him. Back in his office he went over the deeds. The present ownership was marked on a single sheet which contained all the particulars of the property. It was made out to R S Thobani as the two men had claimed.

He held the piece of paper in his hands for a long time, musing over it.

Long before this moment – the like of which he had anticipated many times before – Ebrahim Kanji had come to a conclusion regarding his future. His ambition, all his drive, he realised, had been directed towards a single end: he would never be satisfied until he had gained respect and awe from the men who had violated his father and humiliated him all his life. There were only two ways in which he could do this. He could become powerful in government and make them respect and fear him. Or he could become one of them, only better: richer and more powerful. He had never reached a decision as to which it would be. Now he dearly wished he had spurned the businessmen's initial overture and spared himself the choice.

At the same time as on the previous day, Jaffer Teja was shown in. Ebrahim handed him the deed and Jaffer Teja took it with him. He returned it in less than an hour, inviting Ebrahim to a music party at the Tejas' later in the evening.

That night Ebrahim Kanji collected his first payment.

The London-returned

We still went back for our holidays then and we formed a rambunctious group whose presence was hard to miss about town. We were the London-returned. For two or three joyously carefree months the city became a stage for us and we would strut up and down its dusty pavements parading overseas fashions, our newly acquired ways. Bare feet and Beatle-style haircuts were in then, drawing conservative wrath and doomsday prophecies. We sported flashy bell-bottoms, Oxford shirts and bright summer dresses. And fat pinkish-brown thighs below the colourful mini-skirts of our female companions teased the famished adolescent eyes of our hometown. Come Saturday morning, we would gather at a prearranged rendezvous and conscious of every eye upon us, set off in one large and rowdy group towards Independence Avenue. There to stroll along its pavements a few times over, amidst fun and laughter, exchanging jokes and relating incidences in clipped, finished accents.

The acacia-lined avenue cut a thin margin at the edge of town. It looked out at the ocean a short block away, black and rust red steamers just visible plying in and out of the harbour. Behind it was crammed the old town, a maze of short dirty sidestreets feeding into the long and busy Uhuru Street, which then opened like a funnel back into the avenue. From here Uhuru Street went down, past downtown and the Mnazi Moja grounds into the interior: the hinterland of squat African settlements, the main-

104

road Indian stores, the Arab corner stores – in which direction we contemptuously sniffed, suppressing a vague knowledge of our recent roots there.

On Saturday morning you came to Independence Avenue to watch and to be seen. You showed off your friends, your breeding, your money. It was here that imported goods were displayed in all their glory and European-looking mannequins threw temptation from store windows. And yes, hearts too were on sale on these pavements. Eyes could meet and the memory of a fleeting instant live to fuel one's wildest dreams . . .

We walked among tourists and expatriate shoppers, civil servants and messengers in khaki. And we passed other fugitive groups like ours, senior boys and girls (always separate) from the high schools, who somehow had managed to walk away this Saturday. Our former classmates, many of these. With some I had managed to keep up a brief correspondence. Now some exchanged short greetings, others pretended not to see, and a few turned up their noses with the moral superiority of the uncontaminated. Yet they stoked our merriment no end – these innocents – by their sidelong glances at our mini-skirted companions, or their self-conscious attempts at English accents and foreign manners while sipping iced capuccinos in the European surroundings of Benson's.

It was at Benson's where it began.

She was sitting with a group of friends sipping iced capuccino. They were all in uniform, of course. How can I forget, the green and white, the skirt and blouse? For a brief instant, between two intervening sandy-haired tourist heads, our eyes met. And lowered. And then again a fleeting, fugitive appointment. She had me then.

I think of her as she was then. A small figure, not too thin, with a heart-shaped face: a small pointed chin, high cheekbones, a large forehead. Her hair was tightly combed back and tied into a plain

foamy

pony tail. She sat sipping through a straw, stirring the frothy contents in the tall frosted glass to turn them more liquid. I hadn't heard her voice and I didn't know her. Yet I sat there a few tables away, flustered, self-conscious, saying silly things, laughing uncertainly.

At her table an animated conversation was underway. They talked in Cutchi, not too loudly nor timidly. How self-contained they looked, how comfortable with each other! I felt a little envious, looking in from outside. My subject never looked up again although she must have known I was watching. Presently they waved at the uniformed waiter and went out through the frosted glass door.

We had a word for the kind of state I was in in the few days that followed. Pani-pani: liquid. It means, perhaps, melted. With stylish and refined company – at least as I saw it then – beside me, what made me turn pani-pani at the sight of so plain a figure? The mating instinct, I tell myself a little cynically many years later; how surely it singles out and binds! Kismet, our elders called it. You could walk to the end of the world and not find the right partner, they told you, until your kismet opened up for you. And when it did, as surely and beautifully as a flower, no amount of reason could dissuade you from your choice. In our case it sought to bridge our two worlds. And where else should it strike but on Independence Avenue where these two worlds met.

◇

She lived in what I called the hinterland; not in a squat mud and limestone dwelling but a modern two-storey affair that had replaced it. They were newly rich and moving up; they owned the building and ran the bustling store on the street floor. It had a perpetual sale on, announced by huge signs painted on the walls, pillars, and display windows. And periodically leaflets would be distributed in the area, announcing 'Sale! Sale! Sale!' This much I knew as soon as I came home and gave her description to my

106

sister; it was common knowledge. I learned that she was the daughter of Amina Store. Four times a day an elegant blue hydraulic-suspensioned Citroën sailed smoothly over the potholes and gravel of our backroads, carrying the daughter of the house and her neighbourhood friends to school and back.

◇

On Saturday nights, after a rest from our frolics of the day, we partied. We met on the rooftop of a modern residential building called Noor-e-Salaam in our new suburb of Upanga well away from the bustle of the downtown shops and streets. The latest from the London hit parade wafted down from here. We swung to the rhythms of the Mersey beat while our former friends still drooled over the lyrics of Elvis and Jim Reeves. And to friendly locals we dispensed some of the trendier scraps from our new lifestyles. We talked about nights out in London and trips to the Continent. We introduced new words and naughty drinks.

The Saturday night following my first sight of her I managed to get Amina invited, and also her gang just to keep talk from spreading that I had been stricken. Yet how long can one hide the truth where even the slightest conjecture or suspicion could become truth merely by the force of suggestion? The blue Citroën dutifully unloaded its passengers outside the garden of Noor-e-Salaam and sailed away. They had all come. But I paid attention only to her and what pleased me was that she let me. I had come prepared for the kill, to sweep her off her feet before anyone else realised that she was available. With these unspoilt maidens who haven't left home, I told myself, you can't go wrong with books. And so on the dance floor under a modestly bright series of coloured lightbulbs, while the Rolling Stones sang 'Satisfaction', while we sipped Coke and looked down over the sidewall at the rustling trees and the few people walking on the dark street below, we talked in soft tones about nothing but books. Books!

But it was by her books that my sister swore, a few days later, when she came back from school. Two years younger, she knew I was stricken and had me on the rack, torturing me with bits of information about Amina.

'Look! I swear by holy knowledge!' Brown-papered exercise books held up solemnly as if they meant that much to her.

'Don't lie, or I'll . . .'

'Okay, then.' A mock sullenness. The books are thrown on the sofa. She sits with a long face and draws her knees up close, looks from the corners of her eyes.

'So? What was she asking?'

'But you said I was lying! So I was lying.'

'Come on now, *what*?'

'What will you give me if I tell you?'

'You'll get a slap if you don't!'

'She was asking about you. They are teasing her about you, you know. The news has got around!'

'They are stupid.'

'Well, what do you expect? You danced with no one else. And to talk of studies all the time!' She chuckles.

'I don't know her, silly! What if she is the pious type?'

It didn't hurt, being laughed at like that in the Girls' School. To be studious was still a virtue in those days. No small matter. It was the way out. And it tickled my vanity no end to learn that I had been talked about in a conversation among girls. But perhaps she had found out about me only to reject me?

Because she never came to those parties again. That was the last time, for the entire group. It indicated a certain rejection on her part: of my lifestyle and my friends. She's chosen against me I thought. Perhaps she thinks I'm a loafer. Doesn't she know I go to school, I don't go around London cutting people's hair? I go to school. To have come this close to victory – and to lose out without explanation. Maybe she was teasing, testing me; to show how vulnerable even we could be, the sophisticates who seemed to have the world in the palms of our hands.

What agonising days I spent, keeping a lookout for her up and down Independence Avenue, entering Benson's on impulse and coming out pretending to have forgotten something, a ridiculous figure altogether. There was no way of contacting her; you needed an excuse for that. I could not think of any that would not have seemed a direct proposition. But she could, and she did.

◇

I stand on our balcony looking down on the street. It's five-thirty in the evening or thereabouts. There's not a moving car on the road but some pedestrians are about. Except around noon this sidestreet is shielded from the sun by buildings and it always feels like five-thirty in the evening. A gloomy street. The sun always shines on Uhuru Street a block away. There the heat roasts you and you seek the shelter of the shadier streets.

Below me two boys play marbles on the pavement. Some distance away a figure walks towards them. A circle with a diameter is drawn in charcoal, two marbles placed on the straight line. A game of 'pyu' beginning. I look away to the figure that is closer now and I see it's a girl. Below me a marble gets projected by a forefinger pulled back, lands on the ground, rolls for a while, then takes a sudden turn and sweeps away towards the road – Oh God, it's her! as she walks around them – 'Aaaaaaah!' Rage and disappointment, fists clenched. What did he expect, on such a surface? It's the other one's turn now. My heart leaps: she's entered the doorway of our building. I picture her walking through the courtyard past the boys playing cricket against the wall and taking the stairs. I keep looking down at the road, chest pounding away, face flushed to a fever. Who could she be visiting? – four possibilities . . . no, three . . .

A knock on the door.

'Yes,' says my sister behind me in a voice obviously spilling over with glee, 'he's right here!' I turn away from the balcony and greet her.

She is in a hurry. 'Can I borrow Tranter's book from you? I need it for my revision.'

I bring the book, careful to avoid the mischief in my sister's eyes.

'You can keep it as long as you want – I'll tell you when I want it back.'

'Only for a few days. I have to rush now. Our driver's waiting. Thanks!'

So it was Tranter's *Pure Mathematics* to begin with. She kept it for two months. Meanwhile I borrowed Cooke's *Organic Chemistry* from her, and so it went on. Other books, other excuses, the books untouched. Anything for a chance to meet and talk under plausible cover. Education was not to be tampered with. I would on occasion miss my stroll on Independence Avenue and walk two miles down Uhuru Street with a book in my hand, past the barren grounds, the small dingy shops packed close together, to the flat above Amina Store where she lived. How delicious, luxurious, the anxieties of those days; how joyful the illusion of their pain! They consumed my existence. Her mother fed me hot bhajias when she was there, inviting me in with: 'Come on in, babu, don't stand there in the doorway!' The servant would bring in the delights. At other times her young brother would sit at the dining table doing sums in an old exercise book while we sat on the sofa. I tried sending him downstairs to buy Coke or something, but he wouldn't budge. And the two of us would smile, embarrassed.

People noticed – and they talked, made up their minds. But for us nothing was decided – it could not be – the future was open. This was a chance to be together, to explore the bounds of possibility; and if it lasted long enough, it would lead to an eventuality that was acceptable. But of course, meanwhile, I had to leave. At the end of the holidays, when it was time for me to go back, I asked her: 'Can I write to you?' 'You may, if you want to,' she said. And so we corresponded.

◇

All this is eighteen years ago, and dead: but surely, the dead deserve their due? Or, as our elders said, they come to haunt your dreams.

I sit here in the cosy embrace of a north Scarborough living room in winter, looking out through glass doors, mulling over the last years of our marriage. An intimacy that turned insipid, dried up. Not for us the dregs of relationships, the last days of alternating care and hatred. 'I need a life of my own,' she said. 'I can change; we both can change. You can quit work and go back to college. Is that it?' 'Alone,' she said, 'we've moved apart.' 'And she? – I'll want to keep her.' 'You may, if you want to.'

The open field before me stretches northwards – a vast desert of snow. There are towns out there, I tell myself, cities full of people. Yet I see only endless stretches, a bleak landscape with a few brambles blown by a light wind. And way beyond, beyond which I cannot see a thing, there is a point marked by a pennant strangely still on a short pole. The North Pole as I've always imagined it. In that landscape I see a figure from the past, a former hero . . . Captain Scott from my Standard Six reader, cowering from biting winds . . . Why Captain Scott, out of the blue, as it were and at the wrong Pole? I cannot say for sure . . .

I tell myself I walked too far, too north, and left too much behind. We inhabited a thin and marginal world in Toronto, the two of us. Barely within a community whose approval we craved, by whose standards we judged ourselves the elite; the chic and educated. Our friends we counted on our fingers – and we proudly numbered Europeans, Asians, North Americans. Friends to talk about, not to bring together; points on our social achievement score. Not for us the dull weekend nights of nothing to do. We loved to entertain. And we clamoured for invitations; when we missed one we would pretend not to care and treat ourselves to an expensive dinner instead. We had things to do.

This marginal life she roundly rejected now – just as she did once many years ago. But then she sought me out in spite of it. She came to borrow Tranter's blue and red book though I don't believe she ever needed it . . . and now? She's back in the bosom of Uhuru Street. Or rather the companionship that's moved up Uhuru Street and into the suburban developments of Toronto. Her friends gradually came, one by one, and set themselves up with their families long after we ourselves had moved from London. And it bloomed once more, that old comradeship of Uhuru Street with Amina at the centre – first helping them to settle and then being with them just like old times. Slowly, Toronto, their Toronto became like Dar, and I was out of it.

She came to London exactly a year after the summer in which we had exchanged books and shy but satiated looks in her sitting room, while her little brother pretended to do sums in his warped exercise book on the dining table. This was a time of political change in our country: Asian students from all backgrounds were now desperately trying to go abroad. Her arrival was therefore a surprise; a cousin went to pick her up. A week later, on a Sunday morning, she telephoned me and with heart beating wildly I went to see her. It had been a long wait, a year in which we exchanged letters which delicately hinted at increasing affection. At least I did, and she did not object. I told her I missed her, she reminded me of a funny thing I'd said. I graduated from signing 'Sincerely' to 'Affectionately' and finally 'With love.' She stuck to 'Affectionately.'

She had put up in a hostel on Gloucester Road not far from High Street Kensington run by a Mr Toto, our townsman and reputedly a former valet to an oriental prince. It was a dismal place, this hostel, and I had been through it too. It was your first stop in

London when you hardly knew a soul there. It picked you up and prepared you, sometimes for the worst.

Here you could see what might become of you in a week, a month, a year. Previously it had been more pleasant, a hangout for rich kids, when Mr Toto let you have parties on Saturdays. Now, in the sixties, the faces were more desperate, lonely and white from the cold since they all flew in in September and October. Boys who left early in the morning in home-made Teteron suits carrying attaché cases full of certificates, returning late, hopeless, to a night of exchanging notes on the old, sunken mattresses Mr Toto provided for his iron bedsteads. English pop songs mingled with tear-drenched Hindi film songs, the atmosphere was darkly nostalgic supported by a hollow boisterousness in the corridors. I knew the place so well, its mildew-smelling interior, the migrant Spanish maids in black, landings full of clutter to be picked up, bathrooms stained, taps leaking. I had come here many times, to meet relatives, pick up parcels from home, give advice. Over the years how many must have wept on those soiled, striped mattresses of Mr Toto, prayed on them or indulged themselves in the cold, lonely nights of London!

I entered through the black door with the brass knocker that opened directly onto the street and went straight up to the first floor and knocked on Number One as instructed. There was a shuffle of feet behind the door, which was then opened by a girl in a faded pink home-style nightie with a laced neckline. Behind her, sitting on a bed already made, was my Amina, writing letters. On Sunday you write home I said to myself.

It was still breakfast time and we went down three flights of creaky stairs into the basement. There a narrow pathway through junk and clutter led into a medium-sized brightly lit room laid with blue linoleum, long tables and some benches. There was a steady trickle of traffic in and out of this room and up and down the stairs. Here you could get onion omelettes, cornflakes, and black tea and milk ('English style') from waiters with strangely familiar faces who added advice and humour to the morning's fare.

Later we went out sightseeing. She made her pilgrimage to Trafalgar Square and with her Instamatic I took a picture of her feeding the pigeons to send back home. Then Buckingham Palace and finally Parliament with Big Ben, which for ages had chimed out the nine o' clock hour to us over the radio. 'Eighteen hours, Greenwich Mean Time,' she echoed with amusement in a mock BBC accent.

That night we had dinner at my flat. Rice and curry from a take-away Indian store in Earls Court. After dinner we sat side by side on the sofa to watch television. From the floor below came the sounds of female laughter and hilarity. I knew them well, a group of Asian girls from back home who in their inimitable way mothered the boys they knew. I often stopped at their place and had dinner there. Later I was to introduce Amina to them, but meanwhile I hoped they wouldn't come up to fetch me this night. They didn't and we sat quietly holding hands. Then we went to bed. I slept on my box spring and she on my mattress on the floor. She would not have it otherwise. 'I have to learn to be tough,' she said. For a while we talked in the dark, holding hands. We caressed, touched, our hands trembling, groping for each other in the space between us. Finally the tension reached a breaking point and I looked down in the darkness at the figure below me. 'Can I come down?' I asked, my voice straining. 'Yes,' she said.

How frail our defences, how easily cast aside when the time comes. Nothing could have been more natural. Yet nothing could have shocked more, caused greater pain, in a different setting. How easy it was to judge and condemn from there. Yet no sooner were you here than a layer of righteousness peeled down from your being.

◇

114

The London-returned

Last night we took a drive down Yonge Street, my daughter Zahra and I. We drove among the Saturday night traffic, among the Camarros and Thunderbirds swooping down south for the evening, or just a zoom past downtown, as we'd done before. This time we parked the car and started walking with the crowd, caught by the summerlike festive mood. People waited outside restaurants and cinemas; vendors of popcorn and nuts called out; cars hooted; stores were open and display windows lighted. At Bloor Street we exchanged salaams with a Sikh vendor, then stopped and I bought the little lady some flowers from him. We walked along Bloor Street for some time, arm in arm, talking about our joint future. Fortunately loneliness is not a word in her vocabulary yet. We reached the end of a queue outside an ice cream shop and joined it. We were happy, the two of us. We kept walking on Bloor Street. Somewhere nearby was her mother's apartment; she knew where, but I didn't ask. We reached a repertory cinema where another crowd was queueing and I picked up a schedule. Then, at a whim, I turned on her and asked, 'How would you like to see *Wuthering Heights?*'

Tugging my arm playfully she pulled me along. 'How about seeing *Star Wars?* Finally?'

Refugee

Furtively, he threw another quick glance at the reflection in the window across the aisle. Then a confirming, brooding stare at himself in the window beside him. Through the glass he peered outside at the passing scenery in the dark: ghostly trees and buildings, not a sign of life. When finally he sat back from the darkness, it took moments to adjust to the brightness inside.

There was nothing of interest in the compartment, just the rows of seats and people. Stops were few and far between on this train, passengers who entered and sat down were as quiet as those who got up and left. At one point a big man in a blue suit sat down heavily beside him, barely suppressing a grunt, glanced at him with a look of surprise and turned away to the aisle. Later the man brought out a magazine called *Kultur* and read it, still turned away. In reaction Karim confronted himself in the window yet again, then stared outside. A station flew past that the train ignored. He did not catch its name. It was this unpredictability that was the cause of his anxiety. He had been told to get off and change at Pegnitz.

He was, he had realised unhappily, dressed all wrong. He had bought the right kind of things, of course, and was wearing some of them. All according to fashions picked up from films, tourists, and foreign-returneds. His two sisters, who prided themselves in matters of fashion, had accompanied him shopping; his mother and father had approved his choice. Yet now in the bright light of

116

this train compartment he stood out like a sore thumb, he thought, using an expression he had read from American novels.

No one that he had seen in the train wore sneakers, yet his stood out, sparkling white. His denim jeans were starchy like cardboard, and uncomfortable too. The sweater that in the store in Dar had appeared distinguished and conservative, now betrayed its faded grey, with the three large dirty red and white diamonds in front making pathetic attempts at design and colour. No wonder the first thing anyone looked at was his bright shoes then his face that needed a wash and shave. He looked, felt, so shrunken and small in this strange, alien environment. Alternately he sat forward; leaned back, pressing his arms onto the armrests; arched his back, stretched out his shoulders. He just wasn't right.

◇

He had been instructed carefully. As soon as he got off the plane at Frankfurt not to speak to anybody but head straight for the immigration counters. If anyone came to ask him anything, to offer any help, he was to say only: 'I am a refugee.' To the immigration officers, the same thing: like a prayer. If anyone asked, 'Have you come to look for work?' not to say yes or no, either way to fall into a trap, but to say only, 'I am a refugee.'

He had done just that.

He had got off the plane tired and dazed. The airport was radiant, busy, impressively modern, he expected nothing else. He had emerged into a large open area and paused uncertain: about him human traffic in all directions. He decided to follow a group of fellow-passengers, the wrong ones, apparently, for they soon walked under a lit sign that said TRANSIT. Avoid at all costs he had been told. He stopped, started back in the opposite direction. At that instant, it seemed, two men who had been standing together some distance away started heading towards him. They walked purposefully but without hurrying, their looks fixed on him. Like cowboys walk in movies, he thought fleetingly, as he looked around as if to escape; then he realised he couldn't avoid them and waited. They were the same height, not very tall, one in a dark and the other in a light blue suit, their hair . . . what will they do? He watched them come to a stop.

'Yes, can we help you?' They were standing not very close to him – at a little more than arm's length – but he felt crowded and without meaning to he took a step back but ran into his own bag and stumbled. One of the men leaned forward and took from him the passport he held and flipped the pages, in the process now coming to stand quite close to him.

'I am a refugee,' Karim said.

They tried several questions including the one about work. He stuck to his guns: 'I am a refugee.'

The two men spoke briefly to each other, then started walking away with his passport, and Karim followed. He put his bag down and stopped when he saw a bank of clearly marked immigration counters to his right some distance away. But his interceptors walked on oblivious. He watched their backs, their unforced pace. Then one of them looked behind, and the other turned, and they stopped and looked at him for a moment. They walked back to him.

'I am a refugee,' Karim said, somewhat defensively. There was a pause during which they eyed him reflectively. Then the man who held his passport smacked it with one hand against the other before, to Karim's surprise, handing it back to him. The two went sauntering towards the place where they had picked him up.

An immigration official made out some forms for him, stamped his passport, and gave him an address to report to. He was through.

Then the ordeal began. The few pounds and dollars he had come with he managed to have converted. He had just one telephone number with him, which he had learnt by heart, but he could not make the payphone work. Several times he had to yield it to other, impatient travellers. Minutes passed, he panicked: surely it was not this that was going to undo him? His rejected money tinkled back; the phone buzzed angrily at him; an efficient-sounding operator said something unintelligible to him. Desperately, yet half-heartedly he searched for a face he could trust. But who?

A man walked up to him. He was tall with a greying brown beard, wearing glasses, and grinning with big yellow teeth. His clothes were casual, a tweed jacket over woollen trousers, well used.

'You want to make a telephone call, yes?'

The boy was dumbfounded, alarmed.

'Yes, yes?' The man's insistence did not sound unfriendly though the grin, and the glinting glasses, and the tilt of his head as he spoke gave him a somewhat sinister look.

'I am a refugee.'

'I know that. But you want to make a telephone call to a friend – perhaps a refugee like you – yes, yes?'

'I am a refugee.'

'You are a refugee from where?'

He told him.

'Look, I have been to your country. Yes? I am not an immigration officer as you think. Nor am I a policeman.'

He would not give the man the number he had been trying to call. He had heard too many stories of betrayal, arrived with too many warnings. They sat down and the man bought him coffee.

'I am waiting for someone,' the man told him. 'A writer, not a refugee. Yes?'

Karim nodded. He wondered what he should do. There was one telephone with instructions in English that he had barely tried before being ousted; surely he could make it work after a few more tries? Perhaps he could give someone – this man – a wrong number and learn how to use the phone! But no, if he made up another number he would forget the one he had learnt. That would finish him. He could go to town first . . . but suppose he got lost?

Suddenly the man looked up past him, intently, towards the arrival gate then got up breaking into a grin. Walking towards them was a rotund man with a beard, wearing a corduroy jacket. He looked like an Indian and he was carrying a small hold-all.

'I've got all your information,' said the German, 'except your flight number.'

'Sorry, I forgot. Did you wait long?'

'No, no.'

Karim was introduced to the Indian as the refugee. After a while, feeling rather foolish, he gave the two men the phone number. They talked, had more coffee and the German helped him make the telephone call. It was to a man called Anand in the city of Bayreuth. He was told to go to Bayreuth and given an address.

The German gave him a phone card and told him how to use it. He bought him his train ticket and told him he would have to change at Nurmburg. The train to Nurmburg was 20 minutes late and he might have to go to Pegnitz first and change for Bayreuth. But he should check with the conductor.

It was late afternoon and dusky when the train lurched forward taking him yet deeper into the alien country. The German had found his seat for him, the Indian had waited outside. The few hours of getting to the train station, the looking up of schedules and buying the ticket had been a lively frantic experience. Now left all by himself he began looking around him in the train. It was not very dark outside yet, and superimposed on the fleeting drab scenery outside the window he could just make out the constant but faint reflection of himself on it.

◇

There was a sombreness in the compartment in spite of its brightness, a grim quietude. When he heard a voice it seemed as if

120

it echoed from a distance. It felt eerie because he realised that the train did not move silently but with a steady rumble, which he had to strain to hear through the loud silence. Around him, everyone else sat composed into this stillness, belonging to it, until their stop came and they got up and left.

A conductor came by and clicked his ticket. 'Bayreuth,' he said, pointing at the ticket in his hand.

'Yes. Change at Pegnitz?' Karim asked.

The conductor gave him his ticket, saying a lot of words including 'Bayreuth', and walked away.

Karim looked helplessly around him at the several people who had looked up, then went back to staring out of the window.

He felt strange, preoccupied by an anxiety that allowed no other thoughts, even of home. His one objective was to get himself and his two bags to Bayreuth. There, a phone call or a taxi.

A station came with a name in large letters and 'Bayreuth' in smaller. Obviously this was not Bayreuth. Why put two names to confuse foreigners like him?

Finally PEGNITZ in large letters and some people got up. But he had to be sure. He looked at his neighbour.

'Excuse me, sir. Is this Pegnitz?'

He had to clear his throat and repeat.

The man leaned towards the window and gave a quick look outside. 'Ja. Pegnitz.'

The boy hurried out, pulling his suitcase, the hold-all over his shoulder.

The train disappeared and the station cleared of everyone except him, of all sound except his shuffling. It was overwhelmingly dark. Not a soul, he thought, isn't anyone else going to Bayreuth? . . . With a sinking feeling he realised that the train which had just pulled out was on its way to Bayreuth. That's what the conductor must have said.

Wearily he put his suitcase down against a wall and sat on it. The night was thick with mist. Overhead a sharp silvery half moon sliced through scattered clouds. In the distance, the lights of a town – life somewhere far away – and cars. But not a sound. If something happened to him, if his throat were slit in this god-forsaken place, if he met a ghost or a vampire, no one would know. How stupid, he thought, to venture out like this into the unknown. But he had been pushed out, ever so gently. From a sitting-room full of family in Dar into this utter, utter loneliness under an alien sky.

◇

There was a time, not many years ago, when a bread cart would go creaking down Uhuru Street, pulled by one man in front, pushed by another at the back. It would stop at the street corners and boys or servants would run up and buy bread for the evening or the following morning. Hot steaming loaves huddled in the cart under a green tarpaulin cover. Often at his home they had bread and butter for supper, with sweet creamy tea.

Now there were daily queues for bread and sugar; milk came in packets from the new factory, diluted, sometimes sour. There were rumours that boys would be recruited to fight Idi Amin, the tyrant to the north. And others that Amin would send planes to bomb Dar.

The body of an Asian woman had been found on a beach, mutilated, hanging from a tree. Another, an elderly widow, had been hacked to death by robbers in her flat.

Three times his family's application for immigration to Canada had been rejected. For all three failures his mother and two sisters blamed their father. They were right, his father simply didn't have the heart to pack up his life and move to a cold climate. At each interview he blurted out something that was obviously inappropriate, that raised the interviewer's eyebrows and made the rest of them squirm. Each time though, he had a plausible explanation.

122

Refugee

After the last interview, when they returned home once more without 'medicals', there had been the biggest row. As usual they were in his parents' bedroom that was also the sitting room. His mother was sitting on the bed, braced for the quarrel, his father – resigned to it – was fiddling with the telephone as if unsure whether to make a call or not.

'You didn't have to tell the man that you keep money ready for the robbers – that you joke with them: "Business is bad, next time there will be more" . . .'

'I thought he would like it – think I'm good natured or something.'

'*Good natured*. A fool more likely. You could see the expression on the man's face.'

'The young punk. Come to sit in judgement on us. You know why there is no bread? The Canadians brought a new machine for baking bread at the state bakery. Throw away the old ones they said. Automatic! Well, the machine's broken and there are no parts. Meanwhile someone in Canada's made a bundle. Canadian aid!'

'You've been listening to that socialist again!' His mother practically screamed.

'Shiraz's a clever chap.'

Once more Shiraz Uncle's name entered the home like an evil spell bringing disruption. His father seemed to sense this as soon as he had uttered the name. Shiraz Uncle was his father's educated sister's even more educated husband, and reputedly a supporter of government policies. At the mere mention of his name, Karim's mother's face would contort with rage. Already she was getting flushed and breathless, bosom heaving, searching for words. Sometimes in such a state she got up and went to the kitchen where Karim's two sisters would join her. This time she exploded, pounding her chest twice, saying 'I die! I die!' and weeping forcefully, at which point both his sisters started wailing. His

123

father, who thought he had successfully waylaid his wife's queru-lousness with good humour and a change of subject, was caught off balance.

'What, now?' he began in embarrassment, and looked towards his son to see if even he had resorted to tears.

It was then that the telephone rang, shrilly cutting into the scene, startling most of all his father who was standing next to it.

An operator at the phone exchange had been bribed so his mother could talk long-distance with her family. This was after she kept on complaining about how difficult it was for them to make long-distance calls and how easy for those in Canada. They had a television now, although there was no local TV station and they had to make do with poor reception from Zanzibar. His father even got hold of smuggled foreign goods like cellophane wrapping and soft 'squeezable' toilet tissue and Kleenex. And Avon beauty products for his mother and sisters who in mosque came to be called the Avon ladies.

'Oh the hell we live in!' sobbed his mother over the phone. Her face was wet with the copious tears dripping off her chubby cheeks. At the other end of the line a hushing, comforting voice was just audible. It was usually her brother who called, to whom she was close. After a while his father spoke on the phone, receiving a good ticking off, finally getting furious: 'Call her back if you want to!'

Then surprisingly, like the end of a storm, calmness returned as if nothing had happened and that night they could hear their mother and father talking in barely controlled husky tones in the other room.

His sisters had studied shorthand, typing, bookkeeping and anything else available and were now simply idling, reading Mills & Boon love stories or helping around while waiting to be taken to Canada.

The happiest times in Karim's life had been when one of his

other uncles, his father's brother, had returned with his family from Pakistan after a miserable time there. There had followed happy years, with two families, seven children, living together in adjacent flats. Then his uncle's eldest son who was in Canada sponsored his family; it was only a year since they had left.

His intellectual uncle, Shiraz, had no intention of going to live anywhere else. In fact the government itself sent him abroad several times and Shiraz Uncle always returned, happy to be back, for which many regarded him a socialist fool. But it was Shiraz Uncle who, on returning from Germany recently, told his father of a way to send his son abroad.

'If you want to send him, this is one way, but I don't see why you want to or what's the hurry.'

'I don't think I'll do it,' said his father. 'Karim's never been away. I don't think he'll want to go in that manner. What do you think, Karim?'

Karim was the only other person in the shop, and he said, 'No, I don't want to go like that.' His father was right. He couldn't bear the thought of separation. And his uncle spoke of an indirect route through Germany, where he didn't know a soul

But that evening Karim mentioned the possibility briefly to his mother and sisters, as a novelty, an idea typical of his crazy uncle. But they jumped on it, never letting go for an instant, and he was overwhelmed.

'Your father's no good, you be the man now. God will preserve you. Think of your sisters. Do it for them.'

He had no choice. His silence – brought on by his mother's tender words of solicitation, her trust, her hand on his brow, her quivering lips, her sweet Avon smell – was taken for assent, and they were joyfully discussing the details of his trip when his father entered the room. His mother looked up at her husband in triumph, his sister Yasmin said joyfully, 'Karim says he'll go to Germany.'

Karim looked at him, expressionless. For the first time his father looked beaten.

◇

A warm bright light was shining on his face, making him aware of his unwashed face, sticky neck. 'Polizei' was a German word he understood and the light moved up to a spot above him as a kindness. After some moments he could see the two policemen who were looking at him, telling things to him and to each other. They were quite young and he thought one was perhaps even younger than him.

'Bayreuth,' he said and it seemed that they were walking away, leaving him alone, but they turned and spoke and the younger one came up to him and gestured for him to pick up his bags.

'We go. Police station.'

His heart sank. So be it then. He had been so dispirited, and now, woken up from a dream about home into this bleak deserted train station, he felt terribly depressed. And a trace relieved even at the thought that he would be sent back home.

They drove him to a square brick building which was the police station, walked him to a room at the back that had a table in the middle and some chairs. The door clicked shut behind him and he realised that it was probably unlocked. He sat down on a chair, lay his head sideways on the table between his arms and slept as he had often done out of exhaustion in school.

He was woken up by the sound of a chair scraping the floor. A middle-aged plump woman was wiping the floor with a mop. He watched for a while in amazement. From time to time she glanced at him. After that chore, she began wiping the window panes meticulously. He thought he had never seen anyone wiping window panes before. The room was chilly, the woman was wearing a sweater. The sun was shining brilliantly outside, somewhere, but not entering the room.

When he stood up, uncertainly, the woman left the room in a

hurry, closing the door behind her. A policeman walked in; not one of the two who had picked him up last night: this one was older and plumper, balding. The policeman accompanied him to the washroom. Karim did nothing but stare at himself for a while in the mirror: he felt dull, out of touch with the face looking at him. Not the face he woke up with each morning, excited about the day, taking his time shaving and bathing despite his sisters' pleas to vacate the bathroom, singing joyously . . . If the policeman standing at the door had told him that it was not his face but that of someone else behind him, he would have believed it. Wearily he went back to the room. Two men in civilian clothes were waiting for him. They gave him coffee, examined his passport, began questioning.

This time he readily relinquished the phone number in Bayreuth, and the address. He did not care any more: he did not want to lie, to resist, to stay whatever the cost. He would gladly go back knowing he had tried. The only thing that nagged at him was the thought he had betrayed the men in Bayreuth who had offered to help him. He asked the two officers if he could call Bayreuth to tell them where he was but they smiled.

The men drove him to Bayreuth. Clouds were in motion above, and it was intermittently sunny; the road was a clear grey ribbon in front of them, cutting through greenery in a scene that could have come out of a story book. He wondered if *Heidi* was set in these parts. Perhaps *The Sound of Music*? It all seemed unreal, he could very well be dreaming. They entered town and after a while parked beside some blocks of flats.

On their way to the eighth floor in the last building, Karim wondered if this was really the end, the whole immigration ring to be arrested thanks to him. With trepidation and curiosity and feeling above all like a schoolboy being accompanied to the headmaster's office, he walked between the men who eventually stopped outside a door and knocked stiffly.

There was a short interval and the sounds of some fumbling at the door, after which it was opened, wide, releasing a blast of food smells that stunned him. Karim was gently pushed in by the elbow and had to step over a towel on the floor. There were three men and a woman in the flat. One of the men was an African, from Nigeria, and he was at the piano. The woman, in a mini-skirt, was German. Of the two remaining men, one was from Sri Lanka – Anand, his host – and the other from India. All with papers in order. To Karim the room exuded a homely warmth that was as comforting as an embrace. He wondered how the smell of the cooking had been kept inside, then saw the wet towel that had been used to block the space under the door. The two officers were invited to look inside in the bedrooms and they did. After a peek in the kitchen, they left.

When the two men had been seen to have driven off, pandemonium broke loose around him. The door burst open and five more people – four men and a woman who had been hiding in a German neighbour's flat it appeared – stormed in. And the guest became the centre of attention. Everyone seemed to be speaking at once, asking him questions, skipping his answers, offering advice. They told him not to worry . . . or to start worrying . . . What happened at the airport? they asked, how did the officers get hold of him? what answers did he give? . . . The mini-skirted woman, her face so close to him he could smell her perfume, was telling him, '. . . this is Bavaria. Big feet. Leather aprons. You know? Yodelei-o. Hitler started off here you know . . .'

He didn't know. 'Wagner, Wagner, Wagner,' said the German neighbour and started walking stiffly about the room singing in a bass voice. The second woman had one of her legs on the arm of a sofa and acknowledged Karim's glance with a smile. The Nigerian had started playing the piano. The Indian was walking around looking at wall hangings. A plate was thrust in Karim's hand, he was escorted to the kitchen. Anand was telling him how he could go to Canada via Hamburg.

'You will be let off in a boat some miles from the coast. Throw away your passport. Say you are from Lebanon. Beirut . . . Don't worry. The Canadians can't tell the difference yet. But there is some risk involved, and some money . . .'

All Worlds Are Possible Now

The ships that pass here no longer carry portents of faraway, impossible worlds.

The same harbour, in front of me. The tall-spired grey cathedral behind me on the right. The pipe fence on which I perch, nervous of pickpockets and the traffic screeching at the back of me; a gust of sea breeze to cool the heat still pulsing in my veins after the long walk. Before me a rolling patch of grass down which I remember as a child doing somersaults. And I remember looking up intently at some ship passing slowly through the narrow channel, at the white-clad passengers leaning out gaily against the railings, waving at us. Strangers whose worlds we had no cravings for at that time, mere curiosity.

All worlds are possible now. Shadowy cargo vessels cheerlessly ply these waters, bringers of unaffordable goods, reminders of deprivation, enticements to get up and go. Silent pipers, whom we follow by jet planes, those who can, and stretch ourselves between lives as contrary as the ends of a cross.

I returned, I suppose, because I always returned, ever since those student days I spent abroad. But a broken home also pushed me out as did concern for a palsied father spending his last years alone. There was an element of escape in my return as there was once in my leaving. So what right did I have in proposing, in holding up beggarly promises to someone who'd never made the voyage out even once and was now finally promised the world?

◇

130

All Worlds Are Possible Now

I remember my first day back. I had been brought home the previous night, had been made aware of the new airport road during the drive, a dual carriageway, some other sights, but shutting them out, closing my consciousness, until I had properly set my foot on the ground the next day. After ten years of absence, I had told myself, the reclaiming had to be a ritual, complete, not something done in wondrous spurts. In the same state of wilful unawareness I went to bed under a mosquito net. In the morning walking into the Msimbazi print shop from the back entrance – having walked down the stairs from the flat above – I paid polite tribute to the old Heidelberg still panting out wedding invitations which is all it is good for now. And then, saying my goodbyes I stepped onto the pavement. It was bright outside, reassuringly brilliant, the rude early-morning sun almost instantly roasting the skin and making the sweat glands run. And then, crazed, numb, wound-up, I set off.

I walked down Msimbazi, reached the crossroads at Uhuru, headed straight for it: Amina Store, the name sign no longer above it, only one of the three SALE signs extant outside on the wall, others posted over. I went up the stairs at the side of the building to the second floor; with bated breath, a peep inside the flat through the barred window beside the door: empty. It looks the same; she could have gone to school and her parents could be downstairs in the shop. Or do I imagine, delude myself it is the same? The silence jeers, and I walk down more slowly than I came up. And then, after this ritual, others. Up Uhuru Street – this once beloved street that looks so narrow and small now, I grieve for it. Past shops blaring music that sounds familiar but I haven't heard. It is Ramadhan and men in kanzus and kofias must have come back from prayers somewhere. I hurry past Pipa Store – the corner grocery store where the legendary fat man used to sit, now a tailoring shop, the old shop sign half visible. Past Mnazi Moja grounds, and with beating heart to the street, the building, where I

131

lived as a boy for so many years from whose second-storey balcony
I saw her, Amina, that day – the mother of my daughter as they
say here – but then simply a remarkable girl who came to borrow
Tranter's *Pure Mathematics* from me.

I walked to the second-hand bookstore where Mr Hemani
instantly recognised me as a former Perry Mason fan, went past
Empire Cinema where Mahesh the manager would chase us out of
X-rated Italian James Bond imitations. And then along Ocean
Road, past the hospital, past the Upanga Mosque, to the Boys'
School, making two stops on the way to drink a soda and cool off.

Thus my first reclaiming of Dar. *bring back manner of living*

You say no. Superficial.

I recall the German who sat next to me on my flight back. A tall
man with a huge brown beard, glinting glasses, big teeth. An
incessant smoker. An expert on literature from our part of the
globe it turned out. He heard my story a little impatiently then got
his point in.

'Yes, yes. I would like to recommend a novel. It's called *Time
Reversal*. Yes? *Time Reversal*. It's about a young man – like you –
who returns to his home country, or tries to, but he dies on his way
back. Yes?'

It's fine, I said in my mind, for you to *predict* prognosticate my life.
Next you'll quote me Thomas Wolfe. He did. So now I have to live
according to the dictates of irony, I fumed inwardly, become slave
to an aesthetic. We'll see.

◇

At the Boys' School which was a father to a generation, the tennis
courts were grass-grown, a huge storage shed covered part of the
cricket ground. The halls were quiet when I got there, yet how
could they have competed with the chatter of decades past, the
clamouring voices in my brain. A teacher, a couple of students
looked up curiously as I walked past, a nervous ghost returned to
haunt buildings, impotent against the people inside.

lacking power

132

All Worlds Are Possible Now

In the physics lab a faded certificate hung on a wall in a black wooden frame. A humble-looking document, it could have been a barber's licence. I walked over to it. It was the certificate a former classmate, Nanji, had won for first prize at the annual East African Science Fair. Fifteen years ago. I wondered how many fourth, fifth, or sixth formers, now buzzing in little groups along the benches, would identify with it. Rajabu the lab assistant had been hanging around the school a lot longer. A walking archive, if such things are important. He knew where each of the former teachers went to, under what conditions they had left. He identified me that day, he was one living thing in the school I could clutch on to and I did so desperately. Through him I met the physics master.

The equipment in the lab didn't work. The DC supply at which Mr Bashir, a former teacher, used to stand trembling before turning it on, hadn't been repaired since he ultimately damaged it before returning to India. Old (then new) UN-donated science supplies that needed fixing or installing. I don't know how, I answered the physics master. Wheatstone bridge, potentiometer, simple circuits, perhaps. But atomic physics experiments, those exciting windows to the universe: no.

But perhaps there was a way. I have stretched myself thin after all. I got hold of Lateef, another former student, in Jeddah. Upon secondment from Bell Canada to the Saudi Government, he earns tax-free dollars and avoids the cold; and grinning his naive, good-natured grin he awaits his messiah to take the Muslims out of their misery. I remember standing with him in Toronto outside a Chinese restaurant. Euphoric, happy, stretching out his arms wide: 'Great country, vast. You should see it from coast to coast. Relish it.' Less than a year later he was in Saudi Arabia. For him it was a short hop south from there to Dar. He has come now several times and brought new equipment. He has no hope for the country though. The roads, the schools, the hospitals – every pothole,

133

every malfunction delights him in its confirmation of his pre-
diction. But for this his old school – almost all African now – and
the Asian boys and girls from the other non-government schools
whom he meets after mosque and encourages to see the world, he
is the messiah, and I the philistine.

On one of his visits I took him to meet our former history
teacher Fahndo, now force-retired and living on the charity of a
former student (one of his worst he says) and writing a 'history.' A
secretive Fahndo, this one, much poorer, and not wanting to tell us
what the 'history' is about.

We talked of old times, and Almeida.

◇

We discovered Almeida together, Fahndo and I one day, dying
and helpless. A student coming for extra help got no reply at the
door several days running and, knowing how sick the teacher had
been, assumed the worst. He came to Fahndo: 'Sir, I think Mr
Almeida is dead.'

Fahndo in his brusque arrogant way with students – how well I
remember it – dismissed the observation (it couldn't happen
without his permission). The two had taught together for a couple
of decades. He took me along to Teachers' Quarters to Almeida's
flat. We knocked on the door, and listened. Then holding our
breath we inserted the spare key and threw the door open. And
there he was, the maths teacher, lying shivering in bed. He had
turned a feverish, harried face to look at us. After being jilted in
love once many years ago, Almeida had taken to a beard and grey
clothes and a suffering mien that had been enhanced, it seemed, by
the food shortages several years ago. And since he was the kindest
teacher in school he came to be regarded by students as a
mysterious, saintly and suffering figure.

Fahndo and I found no food in his flat except stale bread and
sugar. But on the kitchen shelves in neatly arrayed ancient boxes
and tins of English crackers and toffees and chocolates we found

134

banknotes, some thousands of shillings' worth. For a maths teacher not to trust banks . . . but then these are uncertain times. Almeida was worried silly that the recently announced devaluation and change of currency would certainly lose him all his life's savings. But Fahndo has connections. It was his patron Nizar who ultimately got the money changed, and perhaps saved Almeida's life, because malaria pills were temporarily unavailable.

One day some weeks later Almeida came to say goodbye to Fahndo. His mother was dying, he said. He should see her. And, perhaps with the money he had saved . . . So he returned to Goa. And found out that he had been tricked: his mother was hale and hearty, his brother wanted to open a bar. Almeida, without an Indian teaching certificate, found a job only with difficulty and according to Fahndo's report cycles twelve miles a day each way to a village school where he teaches.

◇

'So he went home,' I said.

We were in Fahndo's sitting room, two former students come to visit a teacher. Fahndo was extremely flattered, especially by Lateef's visit. He had given us tea brought in by a maid.

'Yes. But what is home?' he said.

Fahndo and Almeida, like many of our other Indian teachers, came to East Africa as young men, unlike most of us, their students, who were second and third generation Africans.

'The whole world is our home. It's a global village,' grinned Lateef.

'This was more his home, I'd say,' Fahndo said reflectively. 'He desperately wants to come back, but who'll let him?'

We went on to discuss other students, friends, classmates. Fahndo takes a great pride in their achievements: professors, scientists, engineers 'out there'. He himself has refused to follow them out . . . and has stoically borne the brunt of the hardships that have swept over the country. *burden*

Finally, as we left, Fahndo wrote something on a piece of paper and gave it to Lateef.

'Here – I want you to do something for me.'

Lateef looked at it, his face lit up and his teeth became visible in a delighted grin.

'Wow. Panjim, Goa.'

'I still have family there.'

'Wow! When were you last there?'

'Long time ago,' said Fahndo with a stern look from his best schoolmaster days. 'Anyway, I'd like to ask you a favour – if you could send some money to my mother.'

'No problem! I might even take it myself!'

As we emerged he asked me if Fahndo was that poor. I told him he couldn't get the foreign exchange without using underhand means, which he wouldn't do.

Again that amused look on Lateef's genial face, as if to say, 'What to do with deluded fools.'

'I see you intend to settle down here properly,' he said, and I simply gave a shrug.

'Take care of her; she deserves the best,' he said at length. He was referring to Farida.

◇

I met her at the mosque one day. I am not religious. That innocent magic, that faith that led you to believe that you had control somehow over your destiny – or at least had a say, a vote, a hand in it – has been buffetted and tattered, like the naive hopes we had of founding a great society . . . But in this city when two hours after sunset the grip of a silent darkness throttles the life out of the day, the mosque is one place that tries to prolong the hum; not with the uproar of previous years; and not at the landmarks that are the town mosque or Upanga mosque but at this once humble one behind the fire station to which we wondered who would ever go.

The mosque has a little library. A room – shed really – its walls impressively lined with books in a bid to provide education where it is at a premium. The atmosphere is appropriately grave, the lighting soft and sparse so that shadows are ominously large, and in the silence the flick of a page can echo sharply as if spurring one to greater concentration. But in fact the books are mostly paperback romance and crime novels that the youth consume in large quantities.

This time as I wandered in there was a boy engrossed among the thrillers, the same boy as on several previous occasions. Several girls walked out huddled over a heap of romances. A librarian absorbed in her own book looked up as I came in, did my quick frustrated hopeless tour and was on the way out. She smiled at me.

I said, 'Don't you have any more books . . . than these? . . .' it was impossible not to give a dismissive wave of the hand. I even threw a look at the book she was reading.

An attractively plain girl with wavy black hair down to her shoulders tied at the back; a striking, long face – white, high-cheekboned, with an oriental quality I had often associated with some Jewish features.

'There are lots of books to read here,' she spoke primly.

Obviously I am not unknown here, it's impossible to be. So she was throwing a challenge.

'But these books are not educational,' I spluttered out an observation she could not possibly argue with.

'Boys and girls need entertainment. We don't have TV here.' Another barb there. unpleasant remark

'And where do they go for serious entertainment?'

'They listen to sermons,' she smiled.

By this time the boy who had been engrossed in the thriller section had come and stood beside her.

'This is my son Karim,' she said, throwing a glance at his acquisitions and a challenging look at me.

We wound up over the course of several days making up a list of 'serious' literature, and we sent it off to friends overseas.

And so on themes of educating children and running a library, we came closer together. The July festival caught up with our shy self-conscious bewildered overtures. We danced the dandia together, that delightful communal stick dance that also allows you to have partners, and between rounds we would sit, drink sherbet, or talk earnestly of our pasts: our failed marriages, our single child each; our aspirations for the future, for her the future of her boy. We allowed ourselves to touch each other.

◊

She is the youngest daughter of Rahim Master, the stern teacher of religion whom at least two generations of 'former boys' remember fondly whenever a verse of a hymn escapes their lips. She was as a girl a serene-looking person, a face of innocence, dressed plainly, walking erectly, two long pigtails falling down to her hips, when other girls were busy with VO5 and beehive hairdos.

Why she was languishing here was the result of a bad marriage that had robbed her of a chance even to go to college: Rahim Master's way of disposing of a daughter with the first decent-looking proposal, at a time when the youth were taking to jeans and western-style dancing. She was living with a brother and his family now, and we were allowed to go out together and given occasional use of the only car. There are not that many men and women of our age here, and such a stage of a relationship implies a successful courtship, a permanence.

That she would impress the grinning, unctuous and rich Lateef was obvious.

I realise that our relationship started out by her humouring my stumbling self-conscious efforts, in the same way we once humoured the good intentions of European teachers. We came quite some way from that beginning. There is a sensitivity in that plainness that penetrates, cuts right through the tangle of convo-

138

luted justifications to the bare longing that lies underneath. Yes, when it comes down to it, there is only a plain longing for a home, a permanence. That is what she taught me. And permanence and home are what I began to hope for and finally looked forward to from her.

It was at the library that Lateef would give his pep-talks to the boys and girls while Farida and I sat at the table waiting for her son to come out inspired. Lateef saw us together and was taken aback; then, face beaming beatifically, he came and shook hands with her.

◇

The ghost of Almeida lies rather strangely over us. I suppose it is because we all knew him and he has only recently left. It's hard not to evoke him cycling with much effort along a country road somewhere.

'Sir,' said Lateef one day, 'tell us what happened to Almeida . . . why did he become – ' he waved a hand, 'this Jesus Christ figure . . . ?'

'He was jilted in love.'

'But why?'

'Why . . . He was about to be engaged to a real angel of a girl, a secretary at D T Dobie. He went on home leave to Goa and the girl was to follow with her mother, so the families could meet and so on.'

'Well?'

'She never went. When he returned, she'd got engaged to somebody else. Rich and influential family.'

Lateef sat back with a grin.

'What are you looking so satisfied for?' I said sharply. My tone caught us all by surprise; I felt angry at myself, and I avoided meeting Fahndo's watchful eye.

This was during Lateef's last visit and I had ample reason for being peevish that day. For one thing, he had been a special hit with the boys and girls. They loved to hear him talk about the Middle East and he thrilled them with stories of how the Arabs lived, about their wealth, arrogance, influence. He had demonstrated the Arab dress to them in the mosque compound, showing off with long strides the white flowing robes and head dress in a circle of enthusiastic onlookers. I took credit for having brought him to them in the first place. Only this time he had come of his own accord, and it was from Fahndo that I found out he was here.

'How can Lateef afford to come here so often?' Fahndo had asked me.

'I wonder,' I replied. 'Perhaps we've seen the last of him for many months.'

'You mean you don't know he is in town?'

It was Friday. When I went to mosque that evening I saw him in the library, sitting on the checkout table talking to Farida.

◇

The second festival of the year – in December – is the lesser one. But this one, over just last night – this morning – was a rip-roaring success highlighted by a public slaughter. Lateef arrived bearing gifts. A wonderful white and blue woollen shawl for Farida. Adidas shoes for her boy who was overjoyed. Shirt and denim jeans for the brother, perfume for the women. Santa Claus from Saudi in a ghalabayeh. I said as much with barely disguised venom at the gift ceremony at the brother's. At the dandia that night he appeared in a dashing embroidered kurta, looking brilliant under the lights, his round face and grin and slight paunch going well with the loose fit. It would have been churlish not to let her play the dandia with him, a generous guest; although intensely jealous, I did try to possess her and lost form.

I had not yet proposed to her, of course. In my reticence I was being modest, but also I did not hasten because I was confident of the prize. Now I saw it slip from me. It was not what she did, the graceful woman, or said, but like a checkmate at a grandmaster's

140

game where nothing is obvious and all understood. If I needed any convincing, I got it when the Adidas-clad Karim let it drop that Lateef had been persuaded by his uncle to stay at their place – why waste money on inefficient hotels?

My game is up. For me now the permanence of this weekly ritual, this breathless empty reclamation of the streets instead.

GLOSSARY

Abunawas   a trickster figure in stories told in Muslim countries
Asian   term used for people of Indian descent
askari (S)   policeman, watchman
ayah   maid
bana (I)   Indianised form for *bwana* (S), used in exclamations, as in 'man!'
banyani (S)   derivative of *banya* (I), name of the Indian trader class
bao (S)   an African board game, played with stones etc
bapa (I)   father
bhajias (I, S)   Indian fried snack (pakoda)
biriyani (I, S)   a rich aromatic dish of rice and meat
bwana (S)   sir
chappati (I, S)   flat Indian bread
chora (I)   'boys' or servants
dahkun (I)   from dakini, a witch or she-devil
daitya Kalinga (I)   the devil Kalinga of an Indian legend
duka (S)   shop
dukawallahs (I)   shopkeeper
Eid   Muslim festival
European   used for white people

ghalabayeh   white robe worn by Arabs
ghee (I)   clarified butter used for cooking
Goan   a native of Goa in India, usually Christian in East Africa
hanisi (S)   impotent; faggot
jambo (S)   how are you?
jamhuri (S)   republic
kanza (S)   long white robe made of thin cotton
Kaunda suit   the type of suit worn by President Kaunda of Zambia and popular in Tanzania
kismet   destiny
kofia (S)   cap
kurta (I)   long Indian or Pakistani shirt
maghrab (I)   dusk
mama (S)   mother; term of respect for an older woman
mhogo (S)   cassava
mnada (S)   auction; market
mshamba (S)   a farmer; uncultured
mzee (S)   old person; a term of respect
nandeali (I)   a prayer for help
pachedi (I)   a light cloth worn over a dress, used to cover the head; can be used as a veil
pina   derivative of pinafore
pipa (S)   barrel
sala (I)   expletive, used for a person, as in 'You!'
salaa (S)   prayer
samosa (I)   a stuffed, fried triangular shaped snack
tasbih(I)   praying beads (rosary)
uhuru (S)   independence
vitumbua (S)   plural of kitumbua, a sweet fried bread